"Authoritative and eminently readable . . . a translation worthy of the original."

Edwin McClellan
Sumitomo Professor of Japanese Studies
Yale University

"I have long been fond of *The Wild Goose*. For more than a quarter of a century I have had an apartment at the top of the Muenzaka slope, where Otama lived and up and down which Okada had his evening walks. No house survives that is old enough to have been hers, but the Iwasaki wall still runs along one side of the narrow street, and people speak of her as if she were real and still among the inhabitants of the neighborhood.

"There is a more important reason than this personal one for being interested in the work. The author is numbered among the giants of modern Japanese prose, and it is among his last exercises in realistic fiction, and probably the best. It is a lively, well-told story the ending of which, unlike endings to much Japanese fiction, is very effective, with the gratuitous happening that spoils Otama's chances for happiness. We must be grateful to have, at length, a full translation from the skillful hand of Burton Watson."

Edward Seidensticker
Professor Emeritus of Japanese Literature
Columbia University

The Wild Goose

Michigan Monograph Series in Japanese Studies
Number 14

Center for Japanese Studies
The University of Michigan

The Wild Goose

Mori Ōgai

Translated with an Introduction by
Burton Watson

Center for Japanese Studies, The University of Michigan
Ann Arbor, 1995

© 1995 Center for Japanese Studies
The University of Michigan
108 Lane Hall, 204 S. State St.
Ann Arbor, MI 48109–1290

Library of Congress Cataloging in Publication Data

Mori, Ōgai, 1862–1922.
   [Gan. English]
   The wild goose / Mori Ōgai ; translated with an introduction by
Burton Watson.
   166p. 23cm. — (Michigan monograph series in Japanese studies ;
no. 14)
   ISBN 0–939512–70–X. — ISBN 0–939512–71–8 (pbk.)
   I. Watson, Burton, 1925– . II. Title. III. Series.
PL811.O7G313   1995
895.6'342—dc20   95–17764
                                                CIP

This book was set in Bembo
Jacket and cover design by Shayne Davidson

Printed in the United States of America

Introduction

Mori Ōgai (1862–1922), novelist, translator, playwright, and critic, was a leader in the Japanese literary world of the early twentieth century. He played a key role in shaping the language and direction of modern Japanese literature, and his works, particularly the novel translated here, have retained their appeal to the present, ranking now as classics of the period.

Ōgai was born in 1862 in the feudal domain of Tsuwano in present-day Shimane Prefecture, the eldest son of a family that for generations had served as physicians to the lord of the domain. He received a traditional-style education in the Chinese classics and Chinese-style medicine and also took lessons in Dutch, the language through which Japan at that time acquired its knowledge of Western medicine. In 1872, shortly after the abolition of the feudal system, his family moved to Tokyo, where Ōgai began the study of German. Two years later he entered the government school that in time would become the Tokyo University Medical Department, receiving extensive training in Western medicine from the German professors who taught there.

Following graduation, he entered the army and embarked on a lifelong career as a medical officer. In

1884 he was sent to Germany to study military hygiene, being among the earliest Japanese students to be sent abroad at government expense. He spent four years in Germany, pursuing his studies under the leading medical experts of the time.

In his student years in Japan he had taken a lively interest in Chinese and Japanese literature and had become proficient in the writing of poetry and prose in classical Chinese. While in Germany, he broadened his literary horizon by reading extensively in German literature and philosophy, as well as in the literature of other European countries. On his return to Japan in 1888, he devoted much time to introducing the works and ideals of Western literature to Japan through translations and essays, as well as to producing original works of fiction and poetry. In his medical career he contributed significantly to the field of military hygiene and nutrition, and in time he advanced to the rank of Surgeon General. As a writer and translator, he became one of the most admired and influential figures of his time.

The story translated here, *Gan* or *The Wild Goose*, published serially in 1911–13, is one of several works of fiction written around this time that draw upon Ōgai's personal experiences. In it he describes the Tokyo of his student days, and much of the interest of the story, both for the author and for his Japanese readers, no doubt lies in its nostalgic evocation of a bygone age, the city and its life as they were in the very early days of Japan's era of rapid modernization.

Within its overall re-creation of the Tokyo of the 1870s and 1880s, the story introduces us to three quite distinct though interrelated worlds. First is that of the students in the Tokyo University Medical Department, Ōgai's own world as he remembered it, exemplified in the hero, Okada, and his friend and fellow student, who narrates the story: a world of young men living in cramped student boardinghouses, combing the secondhand bookstores for something of interest to read, practicing jujitsu, or serving as a member of the rowing team. Educated in the Chinese classics, ornamenting their conversation with allusions to Chinese literature, the students move with an air of ease and optimism, confident of their place in Japanese society and of the role they will one day play in the future development of their country.

A second and quite different world, masculine like that of the students but fraught with harsh realities of which the students are hardly aware, is that glimpsed through the figures of the moneylender Suezō, and the heroine's father, the bumbling and unlucky candy seller. This is the complex world of plebeian Tokyo, where shrewdness and native wit rather than birth and education are what advance one's lot. This world has its links with that of the students—Suezō got his start as a porter running errands for the students, and at the time of the story has advanced to the point where he can act as obliging financier to their youthful follies. But its pleasures are costly and hard-won, with none of the carefree nature of the students' pastimes, and sudden reversal of fortune is an ever-present danger. In Ōgai's hands, both representatives of this world, the moneylender and the candy seller, emerge as subtly delineated characters, far removed in their complexity from the stereotypes of earlier Japanese literature.

Third of the three worlds, and that which seems to hold the greatest interest for the author and to elicit his most telling artistry, is the wholly feminine one inhabited by Otama, the young woman who becomes Suezō's mistress; Suezō's wife Otsune; the sewing teacher and her pupils; and the maids. These are the characters whose mental and emotional lives are explored in greatest detail and who most engage the writer's sympathies. It is their world, with its threatening shadows, its blocks and hindrances, that generates the story's dominant symbols, the wild goose or geese of the closing section— the word *gan* may be taken as either singular or plural— and the pair of caged linnets that fall prey to a ravening snake. And the air of helplessness and despair that marks both Otsune and Otama when we glimpse them last in the end colors the whole novel.

Some readers have objected that so little happens in the story, that there seems so little real interaction among these three worlds, and in particular that the romantic union between Otama and Okada that appears so imminent never comes about. But these flaws, if flaws in fact they are, stem, it would appear, from Ōgai's fidelity to the realities of the scene and era he is depicting. It is always risky to attempt to posit too close a connection between the personal lives of authors and their artistic creations. But at this point I would like to apprise the reader of certain biographical facts concerning Ōgai.

While he was in Germany, Ōgai fell in love with a German woman, an experience that underlies one of his most famous early stories, *Maihime* or "The Dancing Girl." Though his family later attempted to dismiss it as a mere passing fancy, Ōgai apparently seriously considered marrying the woman, and she followed him to Japan after his return in 1888. The army, however, warned him of the damage to his career that such a match would entail, and his mother added the weight of her disapproval, no small consideration in a society as committed to ideals of filial duty as that of Meiji Japan. Ōgai yielded to pressure, and the woman, informed of the adamant opposition of the Mori family, returned to Germany, though Ōgai continued to correspond with her for many years after.

The following year, Ōgai married the daughter of a high-ranking naval officer in a match arranged by an influential friend of the family, but the marriage quickly ended in divorce, enraging the man who had acted as go-between and exposing Ōgai to severe social censure. He remained single for the following twelve years, finally remarrying in 1902 in deference to his mother's wishes. Thus we may be certain that he was acutely conscious of the degree to which romantic attachments and personal freedom were circumscribed by the ideals and mores of his time. This awareness was deepened in 1907 when he published a story entitled "Vita Sexualis," a largely autobiographical account of a young man's sexual awakening and youthful experiences, in a literary magazine. Though eminently restrained by present-day standards, it was frank enough to offend officials in the Home Ministry. Ōgai to his humiliation was subjected to reprimand by the army, and the magazine was withdrawn from sale.

In *The Wild Goose*, written just a few years after this incident, Ōgai depicts Otama's efforts to become intimate with the student Okada as frustrated by a mere quirk of fate, the fact that the boardinghouse where Okada and the narrator live happened to serve a particular dish, mackerel in *miso* sauce, on a particular night. But this is no more than a surface explanation of the ironic course taken by events on that fateful evening.

On a profounder level, Ōgai knew that no liaison between Otama and Okada could be anything but fleeting and furtive, and assuredly could never offer the kind of escape that Otama dreamed of. The worlds of the student and the kept woman were too far apart to permit meaningful contact; the society of the time was too hemmed in by moral and conventional restrictions. If Ōgai was to be truthful in his portrayal of that society, he could hardly end his story on any note other than one of longing and poignant regret.

In 1953, when I was a student at Kyoto University, a movie version of *Gan* directed by Toyoda Shirō appeared. Greatly taken by the film, I set about making an abbreviated translation of the novel, certain that the movie would win international acclaim. It was some years before the picture was sent abroad, however, where it played usually under the title "The Mistress," and I was never able to find a publisher for my translation, though a section of it appeared in Donald Keene's anthology, *Modern Japanese Literature* (New York: Grove Press, 1956). I am grateful to Professor Robert Danly of the University of Michigan for expressing interest in the translation and inspiring me to revise my earlier work and fill in the passages previously omitted. What follows is a complete translation of the novel. An earlier English translation by Kingo Ochiai and Sanford Goldstein entitled *The Wild Geese* was published in 1959

by Charles E. Tuttle Co., Inc. of Rutland, Vermont and
Tokyo, Japan.

Burton Watson

December 1993

The Wild Goose

One

The events of my story took place some time ago—in 1880, the thirteenth year of the Meiji era, to be exact. I remember because at that time I was living in a boardinghouse called the Kamijō directly opposite the Iron Gate of the Tokyo University Medical Department, and in the next room lived a student named Okada, the main character in my story. In 1881 a fire broke out in the Kamijō, it burned to the ground, and I was among those burned out. And the events of the story took place, I recall, in the year before the fire.

Most of the occupants of the Kamijō were students in the Medical Department or patients receiving treatment at the hospital attached to it. Nearly every boardinghouse has one boarder who seems to command an unusual degree of respect. Foremost, he is prompt in paying his bills, and is thoughtful of others in various small ways. When he happens to go down the hall past the room where the landlady is sitting by the brazier, he invariably speaks a word to her, and sometimes plops himself down on the other side of the brazier and chats for a while. If he has drinking parties in his room, he asks her to fix some sort of refreshments, or to do other kinds of favors for him. It may seem as though he is demanding special treatment, but in fact he is giving her a chance to add a little extra to his bill. A fellow of this type usually enjoys considerable respect among others, and hence can do pretty much as he pleases. At the Kamijō the student who lived in the room next to mine enjoyed this sort of privileged position to a quite remarkable degree.

This student, Okada, was just a year behind me and thus was due to graduate before long. If I were to describe him, I would begin by mentioning his unusual disposition. He was a handsome fellow, not of the pale, wispy type, but ruddy-faced and solidly built. I don't recall ever having known anyone with just the kind of face Okada had, though I was friendly with the novelist Kawakami Bizan in his young days, long before the troubles that led to his tragic suicide, and he looked something like Okada. But Okada was a member of the rowing team and much better built than Kawakami.

Though his looks did much to recommend him, they were not the sole reason why he commanded so much respect in our boardinghouse. Above all it was his character and conduct that were impressive. I have known few men who maintained the balance and order in their lives that Okada did. He made no effort to achieve special distinction in his exams, but did what was required carefully and thoroughly so that each term he retained his standing around the middle of the class.

And when the time came to relax, he relaxed. After dinner he invariably took a walk, returning without fail before ten. Sundays he went rowing or on a picnic.

Except for those occasions when he spent the night at Mukōjima with his companions on the rowing team, or when he had gone home for the summer holiday, the hours he spent in and out of his room—and I know because I lived next door—were utterly regular. Anyone who had forgotten to set his watch by the noonday gun could get the correct time by going to Okada's room. Even the clock at the front desk of the Kamijō was on occasion corrected to conform to Okada's pocket watch. Those around him felt more strongly the longer they observed him that here was a man to be relied on. It was this quality of dependability, rather than any lavishness in spending, that led our landlady, never one for flattery, to praise Okada, though the fact that he paid his rent promptly each month no doubt helped. "Look at Mr. Okada!" was her frequently offered advice. To which some of the other student lodgers, anticipating invidious comparison, would retort, "We can't all be like Okada!" Thus, before we knew it, Okada had become the standard by which the Kamijō's residents were measured.

The course that Okada followed in his evening walks was generally the same. Starting out from his lodging, he would take the rather lonely road down

Muenzaka, go along the north bank of Shinobazu Pond, where the blackened waters of the Aizome River flow into it, and then make his way up the hill at Ueno. From there he would wander along the narrow bustling streets of Hirokōji and Nakachō, where the Matsugen and Gannabe restaurants were located, through the grounds of the Yushima Tenjin Shrine, past the corner of the gloomy Karatachi Temple, and back home. Sometimes he turned right at Nakachō and returned by way of Muenzaka. This was one of his routes.

At other times he cut through the campus of the university and came out by the Akamon or Red Gate. The Iron Gate of the Medical Department was shut early, so he entered through the Nagaya gate, the one used by the patients, and got across the campus that way. Later the Nagaya gate was torn down and a new black gate put up, the one that now leads out to Harukichō.

After emerging from the Red Gate, he would go along Hongō Street, past the shop where the man pounds dough for millet cakes while performing feats of dexterity, and into the grounds of the Kanda Myōjin Shrine. Then he would walk down to Megane Bridge, at that time still a novel sight, and stroll a while through Yanagihara on the street by the river that has houses on only one side. From there he would go back to Onari-michi, thread through one or another of the narrow alleys on the west of it, and come out in front of Karatachi Temple. This was another route. He almost never took any route other than these two.

Okada seldom stopped on his walks except to browse occasionally at secondhand bookstores along the way. Two or three of the secondhand bookstores in business at that time in Ueno Hirokōji and Nakachō still exist, and in Onarimichi too there are some from that period, though those in Yanagihara have all disappeared. The ones along Hongō Street have nearly all changed location and owners. The reason Okada never turned right when he emerged from the Red Gate was that the streets in Morikawachō, which lies in that direction, are rather narrow and unpleasant to walk along, but also because at that time there was only one secondhand bookstore in that direction.

Okada's visits to secondhand bookstores were prompted by what nowadays would be termed a "taste for literature." But at that time the new style novels and plays had yet to make their appearance. In the field of lyric poetry, the haiku of Masaoka Shiki and the waka of Yosano Tekkan were a thing of the future. People read literary magazines such as *Kagetsu shinshi*, printed on rice paper, or the white pages of *Keirin isshi*, and regarded the sensuous "fragrant trousseau" Chinese-style poems of Mori Kainan and Kami Mukō as the latest word. I remember because I myself was an avid reader of

Kagetsu shinshi. That was the first magazine to carry a translation of a work of Western fiction. As I recall, it was about a student at some Western university who was killed on the way home for the holidays, and had been translated into colloquial Japanese by Kanda Kōhei. That's the kind of era it was, so Okada's "taste for literature" meant little more than that he read with interest some event of the times that a scholar of Chinese studies had chosen to work up in literary style.

By nature I'm not much good at making friends with people. Even people I met all the time at school I seldom spoke to unless there was a specific reason to do so. And among my fellow students at the boardinghouse there were few that I ever doffed my cap to. The fact that I happened to be fairly friendly with Okada was due to our common interest in secondhand bookstores.

When I went for a walk I did not follow any fixed route the way Okada did. But since I'm a good walker, I managed to cover pretty much the whole area from Hongō down through Shitaya and Kanda, and whenever I came on a secondhand bookstore I stopped for a look. At such times I frequently ran into Okada, and eventually one or the other of us remarked on how often we bumped into each other at such places.

Around that time there was a store on the corner at the foot of the slope leading to the Kanda Myōjin

Shrine that had set out a U-shaped stall spread with secondhand books. One day I spotted a Chinese edition of the Ming dynasty novel *Chin P'ing Mei* and asked the proprietor how much it was. He said the price was seven yen. I asked if he couldn't make it five, but he replied, "Mr. Okada a little while ago said he'd buy it if he could get it for six, so I'm afraid I can't oblige you." As I just happened to have a little extra money with me at the time, I bought the book at the proprietor's asking price of seven yen.

Two or three days later when I ran into Okada he started berating me. "You're a fine one, grabbing up the very book I had my eye on!"

"But the owner of the store said you wouldn't go above a certain price. If you're all that eager to have it, I'll give it to you."

"No need. Since you're right next door, I'll just borrow it when you're finished."

I agreed to that, and that was how Okada and I, neighbors who up to then had had little to do with one another, became friends.

Two

At that time the Iwasaki mansion already stood on the south side of Muenzaka, though it was not enclosed by a towering mud rampart as it is today, but by a dingy stone wall that sprouted ferns and horsetails from the crevices of its moss-covered slabs. I do not know to this day whether the area above the stone wall is flat or hilly, since I have never been on the grounds of the Iwasaki estate, but at that time one could tell it was thickly overgrown with trees because their roots were visible from the roadway. The roots were in turn overgrown with weeds that were seldom mowed.

Along the north side of the sloping street stood a row of shabby houses, the most presentable surrounded by a board fence, the others the sort of places occupied by craftsmen. The only shops were one or two places selling tobacco or hardware. Attracting the attention of the passerby halfway up the hill was the home of the sewing teacher, with its crowd of girls sitting by the lattice window at their work in the daytime. In nice weather when the window was open and we students would pass, the girls would all look up from their work to watch us go by before resuming their chatter and laughter.

Passing by in the evening, one might notice a little house next door with a clean-wiped lattice door and the granite flags that paved the entranceway freshly wet with water to keep down the dust. On cool evenings the paper panels of the house were shut; in warm weather its windows were hung with bamboo blinds. Beside the bustle of the sewing teacher's house next door, it seemed conspicuously hushed and still.

It was September of the year of my story, and Okada had gone for his usual walk after dinner. He was strolling down Muenzaka when he happened to notice a woman returning from the public bath enter the lonely house next to the sewing teacher's. The weather was fallish, already too cool for anyone to be sitting outdoors. As Okada came down the deserted street, the woman arrived before the lattice door of the house and was about to open it when, hearing the sound of his wooden clogs, she stopped abruptly and turned in his direction. She was wearing a summer kimono of dark blue crepe tied with a sash of black satin and tea-colored facings, the slim fingers of her left hand holding a bamboo basket of toilet articles, her right hand resting on the door. The figure of the woman as she turned to look at him made no deep impression on Okada, but for a moment the details of her image lingered in his eyes—the hair freshly done up in gingko-leaf style, sidelocks thin as the wings of a cicada, the high-bridged nose, the rather melancholy face that seemed somehow from the forehead to the cheeks a little too flat. But it was no more than a momentary perception, and by the time he had descended to the foot of the slope he had completely forgotten her.

Two days later, however, when he again headed toward Muenzaka and drew near the house with the lattice door, he suddenly recalled the woman he had met coming back from the bath, and he turned to look at the house. It had a bay window fitted with a grating of bamboo uprights and two thin, vine-entwined horizontal strips of wood. The sliding paper panels of the window had been opened about a foot, revealing a pot with lilies growing in it. He slowed his pace a little to be able to observe more closely, and as he arrived directly in front of the house, all at once, above the potted plant, from the background that until then had been lost in gray darkness, a pale face appeared. Moreover, the face looked at him and smiled.

After this when Okada passed the house on his walks he almost never failed to see the face of the woman. She began to insinuate her way into his idle imaginings, and in time made herself quite at home there. He wondered if she waited for his passing, or was merely gazing idly out the window when she happened to meet his glance. He tried to think back to the time before he had met her returning from the bath and to remember whether he had seen her face in the window then, but he could recall only that the house next to the sewing teacher's, the liveliest on the street, had always been very clean and lonely. He had doubtless wondered what sort of person lived there, but had come to no conclusion. The paper panels of the window had always been shut, the blinds lowered, and the interior of the house completely silent. In view of all this, he finally concluded that the woman had only recently begun to take an interest in what went on in the street outside, and had opened the window in anticipation of his passing.

Seeing her each time he passed, and thinking of her from time to time through the day, Okada gradually came to feel quite friendly with the woman in the window, and some two weeks later, as he strolled by one evening, he unconsciously raised his cap in greeting. The dim white face flushed red and the sad smiling countenance broke into a lively grin. After this Okada always doffed his cap to the woman in the window.

Three

Okada had a great fondness for the *Yü Ch'u hsin-chih*, a collection of Chinese essays and stories, and one of the items in it, "The Big Iron Bludgeon," a tale of military prowess, he could all but recite from memory. It had long been his ambition to become adept in one of the martial arts, though he had never had an opportunity to do so. In the last few years, however, he had taken up rowing and had gone at it with such enthusiasm that, at the recommendation of his teammates, he had been made a member of the rowing team.

There was another work in the *Yü Ch'u hsin-chih* that Okada liked to read, "The Life of Little Blue," a story of a beautiful but ill-fated young woman. The women featured in Chinese tales of this sort would, to put it in somewhat novel fashion, keep the angel of death himself waiting on their threshold until they had meticulously applied their powder and makeup. Such women, for whom beauty was their very life, moved Okada deeply. He viewed women in simple terms, as beautiful beings, lovable beings, who could be content in any setting whatever; and their beauty and lovableness he felt it was his duty to guard and protect. In the course of reading poems in "fragrant trousseau" style that dwelt on feminine charm, or the sentimental and fatalistic romances of the Ming and Ch'ing litterateurs, he unwittingly fell deeper and deeper under the spell of such ideas.

Though considerable time had passed since Okada first began greeting the woman in the window, he had made no attempt to find out anything about her. Needless to say, the appearance of the house and the way the woman dressed strongly suggested that she was someone's mistress, but that did not particularly bother him. He did not know her name, nor did he make an effort to learn it. It had occurred to him that he could find it out by looking at the nameplate on the house. But he hesitated to do so when the woman was at the window, and even when she was not, he was concerned about what the neighbors or passersby in the street might think. So in the end he never looked to see what name was written on the little wooden plaque that rested in the shadow of the eaves.

Four

I did not learn the full history of the woman in the window until some time after the events of my story, which centers on Okada, had taken place. But it may be convenient to relate it briefly here. It begins at a time when the Medical Department of the university was still located in Shitaya. At that time the gatehouse of the old Tōdō estate, a building whose walls were checkered with plastered inlays of gray tile and pierced by windows fitted with vertical wooden bars the thickness of a man's arm, served as a dormitory. There, to put it in rather unflattering terms, the students lived penned up like so many wild beasts. Today the only such windows still in existence are those in the turrets of the old Edo Castle. Even the bars on the lion and tiger cages in the Ueno Zoo are flimsy by comparison.

At the dormitory were porters, dressed in *hakama*-type trousers of duck with white cotton waist bands, who ran errands for the students. The items the students most often sent out for were *yōkan* and *kompeitō*. For those interested in cultural history, it may be worth noting that the former refers to roasted potatoes and the latter to parched beans. Porters fetching such items received two sen per errand.

Among the porters was one named Suezō. While the others went around with their mouths gaping stupidly and their beards grown out like chestnut burs, this fellow kept the lips of his clean-shaven face tightly clamped. And whereas the duck trousers of the other porters were often soiled, Suezō's were spotless, and sometimes he appeared wearing clothes of some superior fabric, with an apron to keep them from getting soiled.

I do not recall from whom or just when I first heard it, but people used to say that if you were out of money you could get Suezō to advance you some. At first, it seemed, he only lent out small sums like fifty sen or one yen, but gradually he began to lend five or ten yen at a time, and to require an IOU from the borrower, writing out a new one when an extension of the loan was needed. Soon he had become a full-fledged moneylender.

What had he used for capital when he began? Surely he must have had something more than the meager two sen tips he had put away. But when the full energy of a human being is directed toward a single goal, there is perhaps nothing that is impossible. In any event, by the time the school moved from Shitaya to Hongō, Suezō was no longer a porter. A steady stream of students who had been improvident in their spending now sought him out at his new home on the edge of Shinobazu Pond.

When Suezō became a porter, he was over thirty and, poor though he was, already had a wife and children. After he made a success of moneylending and moved to the edge of the pond, he began to feel extremely dissatisfied with his homely, quarrelsome wife. It was then that he remembered a girl he used to see from time to time when he came through the streets from Neribeichō on his way to the university.

Threading along an alley lined with broken gutter boards, he would pass a dimly lit house, its door always half shut and, in the evenings, a pushcart parked under its eaves, making the alley, narrow to begin with, so crowded one could not pass without turning sideways. It was the sound of someone practicing the samisen that first attracted his attention. The owner of the instrument, he discovered, was an attractive girl of sixteen or seventeen who, in spite of the poverty of her surroundings, always appeared fresh and neat and attired in a clean kimono. If she happened to be standing in the door when anyone passed, she would invariably withdraw in haste to the dim recesses of the house. Suezō, alert to everything around him, soon learned through chance that the girl's name was Otama, that her mother was dead, and that she lived alone with her father, who sold little candies fashioned in fanciful shapes in a stall in Akihanohara.

Sometime after acquiring this information, Suezō became aware of a revolutionary change in the house. The pushcart was no longer parked by the eaves at night. The little house and its surroundings, usually so quiet, had, it seems, to use the phraseology of the time, entered upon an "era of enlightenment." The warped or broken gutter boards were replaced, the entranceway was made more sightly by the installation of a new lattice door, and at one point Suezō spied a pair of Western-style shoes in the doorway. Not long after, a new nameplate appeared by the front door bearing the name of Officer So-and-so of the police force. In the course of his shopping errands in Matsunagachō and Nakaokachimachi, Suezō learned, once more by chance, that the old candy seller had acquired a son-in-law, the policeman whose name appeared at the door.

Otama was more precious to the old man than life itself, and to hand her over to some fierce-looking officer of the law seemed more dreadful than having her snatched away by goblins. And he was appalled at the thought of such a son-in-law actually moving into the house with him. Before agreeing to the arrangement, therefore, he discussed it with a number of persons he had known over the years, but not one of them advised him in so many words to reject the policeman's proposal of marriage. Some chided him for having turned down perfectly good marriage proposals in the past, claiming that he could not bear to part with an only daughter, yet now he was confronted with an offer that was all but impossible to refuse. Others said that if he could not bring himself to agree, the only alternative was to move somewhere far away, though they warned that, since the other party was a police officer, he could doubtless find out at once where the old man had moved and go after him. So in the end even running away was out of the question.

One of the nearby housewives whose judgment was held in high esteem was said to have told him flatly: "A lovely girl like Otama, her samisen teacher praising her and saying she has all sorts of promise—didn't I tell you to send her off as soon as possible to be trained as a geisha? When an unmarried policeman comes from house to house looking for a wife, if you have a pretty daughter at home, he's going to make off with her whether you like it or not. It's just your bad luck that that's the sort of fellow who spotted her—you have to make the best of it!"

About three months after Suezō heard rumors of these happenings, he one morning noticed the door of the old candy-seller's closed and a sign posted on it that read: "House for rent. Inquire at west edge of Matsunagachō." Picking up bits of gossip in the course of his shopping, Suezō learned that the policeman already had a wife and family back home in the country. They had suddenly turned up without warning and there had been a fearful row. Otama had dashed out of the house, declaring she was going to throw herself down the well, and had been stopped just in time by the wife next door, who had overheard what was going on.

When the old man was first considering the policeman's proposal, he consulted various people, but none were the sort who could give him advice on the legal questions involved. He had not the slightest idea what steps had been taken to register the marriage or file the necessary official notifications. When the policeman, stroking his moustache, had said he would take care of all such matters himself, the old man had accepted his word without the least suspicion.

At that time there was a grocery store in Matsunagachō called Kitazumi. The daughter of the owner, a pale, round-faced girl with a chin so recessive that the students referred to her as "Chinless," remarked to Suezō, "I really feel sorry for Otama! She's so trusting a soul she thought she had a real husband, but for the policeman it was just a place to spend the night!"

"It's a shame about the old man too," added the proprietor of the store who was standing nearby. "He said he was too ashamed to face the neighbors anymore and so he moved all the way to Nishitorigoe. But none of the children in that neighborhood have ever been his customers, so he still goes to his old location in Akihanohara to set up his candy stall. At one point he even sold his pushcart. It was on sale in a secondhand furniture store in Sakumachō, but he explained to the man what had happened and got it back again. With all that and moving his house too, it must have cost him quite a sum—more than he can afford, I'm sure. The policeman went off leaving his wife and children in the country to fend for themselves while he drank saké in town and acted big. He even had the old man, who was never a drinker, keeping him company. For a while the old man must have thought he was dreaming, living the life of a retired gentleman!" exclaimed the proprietor, rubbing his bald head.

Given Suezō's now much widened circle of acquaintances, it was easy enough for him to make inquiries around Nishitorigoe; they revealed that the old man was now living next to the rickshaw shed back of the Ryūsei Theater. His daughter was with him. Someone was sent to inform them that a certain prominent merchant wished to make Otama his mistress and to sound them out on the matter. At first Otama objected to becoming a mistress, but she was by nature an obedient young woman, and she was strongly urged to think of the benefits that such an arrangement would bring to her father. Eventually it was agreed that she would meet with the gentleman at the Matsugen Restaurant.

Five

Ordinarily Suezō thought of little else than money matters, but before he had even ascertained Otama's whereabouts or whether she would agree to his proposal, he had begun looking around for a house to rent somewhere in his neighborhood. After considering a number of possibilities, he found two that were to his liking.

One was situated on the edge of the pond, halfway between the home of the writer Fukuchi Gen'ichi-rō, which was next to his own home, and the Rengyokuan, a restaurant famous for its buckwheat noodles. It was situated just beyond the southwest corner of the pond, in the direction of the Rengyokuan, and was set back a way from the street. Just inside the bamboo fence grew a Chinese black pine and two or three arborvitae trees, and beyond their branches one could glimpse a bay window fitted with a bamboo lattice.

The house had a "For Rent" sign on it, but when Suezō made inquiries he discovered that it was still occupied. A woman of about fifty showed him around the premises. Her husband, she explained, had been chief retainer to a daimyo of western Honshu, but after the abolition of the feudal system he had been employed as a minor official in the Finance Ministry. He was well over sixty now, she said, continuing to volunteer information on the subject, but a great stickler for appearances. He would tramp all over Tokyo looking for a newly built house to rent, but after he had lived in it a while and it had started to show the least sign of wear, he would insist on moving somewhere else. Their children had of course grown up and left home long ago, so the house wasn't subject to rough wear, but still a house gets old and the shoji panels have to be repapered and the tatami mats replaced. Rather than bother with all that, however, he preferred to move someplace new.

The woman rattled on in this fashion, apparently so peeved at her husband's incessant moving that she felt compelled to air her annoyance even before a complete stranger. "This house is perfectly clean and neat, as you can see, but already he wants to move out!" she exclaimed as she showed Suezō around the house. The rooms were in fact all in quite good shape and Suezō, favorably impressed, made a note of the rent, deposit money, and rental agent in his pocket notebook.

The other house that appealed to him was a smaller place about halfway up the slope of Muenzaka. There was no sign on it, but Suezō happened to learn that it was up for sale and went to take a look. It was owned by a pawnbroker in Yushima Kiridōshi whose parents had lived there in retirement until very recently, when the father had died and his widow moved to her son's house. The place next door, occupied by a sewing teacher, was rather noisy, but the house had been built expressly for the elderly couple and the wood used in it selected with care. Somehow it looked as though it would be very comfortable to live in. From the lattice front door down to the entrance garden flagged with granite, everything contrived to give a feeling of neatness and refinement.

For a whole evening Suezō, tossing this way and that on his sleeping pallet, debated which house to choose. Beside him lay his wife Otsune, who had lain down with the children in order to lull them to sleep and had dropped off to sleep herself. Her mouth was wide open and she was snoring robustly. Suezō commonly stayed up until all hours mulling over his moneylending affairs, and his wife had long ago ceased to pay any attention to whether he was still awake or not.

Staring at his wife's face, Suezō mused over the oddness of the situation. Who'd suppose there could be a woman with a face like that! he thought. Otama now— it's been a long time since I saw her. She was hardly more than a child then, but quiet as she was, there was something sprightly and charming about her, the kind of face you couldn't resist. And by now she must be more fetching than ever. I can hardly wait to see what she looks like!

And here's this old woman of mine, sleeping away brazen as ever. If she supposes I never think of anything but money, she's badly mistaken. Look there—the mosquitoes are out already! That's what I hate about living in Shitaya. Time to get out the mosquito net. It doesn't matter about the old woman, but I don't want the kids eaten alive!

Then his thoughts turned once more to the question of the house. Pondering the pros and cons of the situation, it was past one o'clock before he finally reached a conclusion of sorts. Some people might say that the house by the pond is best, what with the nice view and all, he thought. But I get all the view I want from this house. The rent is cheap, but rented houses can be a headache. And anyway, it's in too open and exposed a location, where people are likely to notice it. What if I happened to open the window just when the old woman was going by with the kids on the way to Nakachō? If she spotted me, it could mean real trouble.

The Muenzaka place is a bit gloomy, but almost no one passes that way except perhaps some students out for a walk. Laying out a lot of money at one time to buy it might seem risky, but the price is cheap considering the quality of the wood that's in it. And if I take out insurance on it, I can get back my original investment anytime I want to sell it—no worry there. Yes, it better be the Muenzaka place!

Then in the evening, after I've been to the bath and changed into some better looking clothes, I'll think up some tale to tell the old woman so she won't suspect anything, and off I go! What will it be like, when I open the lattice door and step inside? There will be Otama, a kitten or something on her lap, sitting there lonely, waiting for me to come! Of course she'll be carefully made up. And I'll see she has whatever she wants in the way of kimonos. . . .

But wait a minute! No use throwing money away! You can get perfectly good items at the pawnshop. Why act the fool by lavishing kimonos and hair ornaments on a woman the way other men do? Look at Mr. Fukuchi next door. He lives in a house bigger than mine and goes parading around the pond with geishas from Sukiyamachi, showing off and making the students envious, but actually he's up to his ears in debt. He gets by because of the tricky things he writes, but if a store clerk tried those kinds of tricks he'd be fired in a flash!

Now I remember—Otama plays the samisen. Maybe she'd pluck the strings with her finger and sing a love song to put us in the mood. But then, outside of that episode of the policeman, she doesn't know anything about such worldly matters. She'd say she didn't want to play because I'd laugh at her, and even though I urged her, still she'd hold back. Whatever it was, she'd go about it in a bashful way, turning red in the face and squirming around. Think how it would be, the very first evening I went to see her . . .

So Suezō's imaginings darted off first in one direction, then in another, never coming to rest, till nothing remained of them but a shimmer of pale skin and a whispered voice, and Suezō drifted off into pleasant slumber. Beside him, his wife continued her snoring.

Six

The meeting at the Matsugen Restaurant was for Suezō a festive occasion. People speak in general terms of penny-pinchers, but in fact there are many varieties of the breed. All share in common a nature particularly attentive to the little points of saving that causes them to tear a sheet of toilet paper in half before using it, or to attempt to conduct business by postcard rather than letter, writing in characters so small that one must use a magnifying glass to decipher the message. But while some will pursue this stifling frugality throughout every aspect of their lives, others will, as it were, leave themselves some little hole through which to breathe. The misers portrayed in fiction and drama up to now have usually been of the former, uncompromising type. Real life specimens, however, are often quite different. Tight as they may be in some matters, they will make vast exceptions where a woman is concerned, or be unaccountably lavish when it comes to food and drink.

As noted earlier, for Suezō it was one of the pleasures of life to maintain a clean and neat appearance. While he was still a porter at the university, he would on holidays exchange his customary tight-sleeved cotton coat for the fine kimono of a merchant, so that students meeting him by chance on such occasions would stare in astonishment at his silken-clad figure. Beyond this delight he took in his appearance, however, he had no particular diversions or extravagances. He was involved in no intrigues with geishas or prostitutes, nor did he spend his time dining and drinking about town. A bowl of noodles at the Rengyokuan was a big splurge for him, and until recently his wife and children had never been invited to accompany him on such occasions.

He considered it unnecessary to have his wife's appearance match his own. When she would plead with him to buy her some item, he would advise her curtly not to talk nonsense. "You're not like me," he would add by way of explanation. "I have appearances to keep up, contacts to maintain, so I am obliged to dress like this!" After he began to be better off, he occasionally went to some restaurant for dinner, but always with a group; he never went alone. When he made the arrangements to meet Otama, however, he was suddenly taken with a mood of festive ostentation and gave instructions that the meeting was to be held at the Matsugen.

But before the meeting could take place, there was one problem that had to be dealt with, that of the clothes that Otama was to wear. If it had been just Otama, there would have been no difficulty, but as it turned out, clothes had to be provided for her father as well. Even the glib old woman who was acting as go-between in the arrangements found herself stymied on that point, as she realized that Otama would invariably second her father's stand on any matter, and that if pressure were brought to bear to keep the old man away, all the negotiations could end in failure.

The old man's position was this. "Otama," he told the go-between, "is an only daughter and very precious to me. Moreover, my case is somewhat special because she is the only close kin I have. My wife and I went along with just the two of us, but when she was over thirty she had a child, Otama, and died soon after of complications. I had to find someone to nurse the child. And then, when Otama was only four months old, she came down with the measles that was raging all over Edo at the time. The doctor gave her up for lost, but I dropped my business and everything else and nursed her till I pulled her through at last.

"The whole world was in an uproar then; it was two years after Lord Ii was assassinated, the year the Westerners were cut down at Namamugi. Later I lost my shop and everything I had. Any number of times I was on the point of killing myself, but I would look at Otama, her little hand fumbling at my chest, gazing up at my face with those big eyes and smiling, and I knew I could never bring myself to kill her too. So I went on somehow bearing what I thought I couldn't bear, living from one day to the next.

"I was already forty-five when Otama was born, and looked even older because of all the trials I'd been through. People bent on being helpful would remind me of the proverb that 'Two can live on what won't do for one'; they offered to introduce me to a widow with a little money who was looking for a husband, or urged me to turn Otama over to her mother's people. But Otama was too dear to me—I refused to listen to such talk.

"But as they say, poverty makes for a dull head. After all the care I'd taken in bringing her up, I went and handed her over to that two-faced liar of a policeman to be his plaything! It makes me sick with rage every time I think of it! But still she's a good girl, as everyone admits, and I want to see her married to someone upright and proper. With a father like me, though, who'd be willing to have her?

"Whatever happens," he insisted, "I don't want to see her become somebody's mistress or kept woman. But you tell me that this gentleman of yours is perfectly trustworthy. Otama will be twenty next year and it doesn't do to put such things off too long. So I guess I'd better listen to your proposal. But since she means so much to me, I want to be sure to go along when she meets the gentleman."

Suezō was anything but delighted when he heard of these remarks; it was apparent that things were not going as he had hoped. Once Otama had been escorted to the restaurant, Suezō had intended to dismiss the old woman as quickly as possible so he could enjoy Otama's company alone, but this was something quite different. With her father tagging along, it was turning into an unexpectedly gala affair.

Of course Suezō had meant it to be a gala affair for himself since it marked the first step toward the realization of his long-cherished hopes. But only a cosy tête-à-tête between Otama and himself would do to celebrate such a happy occasion, he felt. Now if her father joined in, the whole nature of the festivities would be seriously affected.

The old woman had emphasized to Suezō that Otama and her father were rather straitlaced, and that in the beginning both had been adamantly opposed to any suggestion that Otama become a mistress. The old woman had managed one day to call Otama out of the house and meet with her alone, and at that time had impressed on her that her father could not go on working forever and inquired if she didn't wish to make things easier for him. She went on to elaborate on all the advantages of the arrangement until Otama had finally agreed. It was only after that talk that the father had been brought around.

Listening to this report, Suezō was secretly pleased to think that the woman soon to be his was of such an unselfish and obedient nature. But with both father and daughter so straitlaced, the meeting at the Matsugen would be more like a young man presenting himself for inspection by a prospective father-in-law. The "gala occasion" having taken such a strange turn, Suezō felt as though his earlier ardor had been doused with cold water.

But he had chosen to have himself represented as an affluent businessman, and now he felt obliged to live up to the role. So to demonstrate his magnanimity, he agreed to provide appropriate apparel for both Otama and her father. It occurred to him that once Otama was in his hands, he could not very well ignore the needs of her father, so in a sense he was simply supplying goods beforehand that he would have to supply sooner or later anyway. This thought helped him to reach his decision.

Normally in such cases one would merely hand over to the other party an appropriate sum of money, but that was not Suezō's way. Being so particular about his appearance, he had his own tailor to look after his needs, and he now instructed this man to prepare proper attire for his two guests. Before this could be done, however, the old woman acting as go-between had to be sent around to determine the measurements of Otama and her father. I regret to add that this procedure of

Suezō's, so typical of his wily and parsimonious habits, was completely misinterpreted by Otama and her father, who took it as a sign that he respected them too highly to risk offending them by crassly offering them cash.

Seven

Few fires have broken out in the vicinity of Ueno Hirokōji and I do not recall hearing that the Matsugen burned down, so for all I know the very room where the meeting took place may still be in existence. Suezō, having requested a small quiet room, was guided down the hall from the entrance on the south and shown to a six-mat room on a corridor to the left. There a man dressed in the uniform of the restaurant was busy rolling up a large paper blind.

"I'm afraid until it gets a little later the evening sun will be coming in like this," the maid, who had shown Suezō in, apologized before withdrawing. Suezō sat down, his back to the alcove with its ukiyoe scroll painting and little vase of jasmine, and scrutinized the room carefully.

Since it was a ground-floor room, it would ordinarily have looked out on the street that runs along the edge of the pond and the unsightly area just beyond that had formerly been a horse racing track but had subsequently been converted for use in bicycle races. To prevent people from looking in, however, a fence had been constructed between the restaurant and the street, thus unfortunately shutting out the view of the pond. The area between the building and the fence was too narrow for a proper garden, but from where Suezō sat he could see two or three pagoda trees in a clump, their trunks as shiny as though polished with oily rags, and a stone lantern. Other than these, there was nothing to be seen but a scattering of little cedars. The evening sun continued to beat down, and beyond the fence clouds of white dust rose from the feet of people passing along the street, but inside the fence the moss shone a cool green from the water that had been sprinkled on it.

Presently the maid returned with tea and a coil of incense to keep off the mosquitoes and asked for his order. He explained that he would order after the other members of his party had arrived and, sending her away, settled back to smoke alone. When he first sat down he had thought it was rather hot. But before long a gentle breeze began to blow in now and then from the hallway, bringing with it various odors from the kitchen and other parts of the restaurant, and he felt no inclination to pick up the dingy paper fan that the maid had placed by his side.

Leaning against the pillar of the alcove and puffing rings of smoke, he began to imagine what the meeting would be like. The girl that he had thought so charming when he used to catch a glimpse of her as he passed by had been, after all, only a child. What sort of woman had she turned out to be? How would she look when she appeared? Her father would be coming along too. What a nuisance! Wasn't there some way to get rid of the old man quickly? From upstairs came the sound of someone tuning up a samisen.

Suezō heard the footsteps of several people in the corridor. "Your guests have arrived," announced the maid, sticking her head in at the doorway.

"Come now, step right along in. The gentleman is very amiable and there's no need to stand on ceremony!" It was the old go-between speaking in her shrill, cricket's voice.

Suezō rose hastily from his seat and stepped into the hall, where the father stood bowing and hesitating by the wall where the corridor turned. Behind him was Otama, not looking at all intimidated but gazing around in curiosity. The plump-faced, attractive child had grown into a graceful woman, her hair done in a neat gingko-leaf coiffure, her slender face not heavily made-up, as one might expect on such an occasion, but almost unadorned. If she was quite different from what Suezō had imagined, she was more beautiful, and as he eagerly eyed her form he experienced a feeling of profound satisfaction.

As for Otama, since she was to sell herself to spare her father hardship, she had made up her mind that it was of little importance who the buyer might be.

But perceiving the affable look in Suezō's keen dark eyes, and noting the elegance and refinement of his attire, it suddenly seemed to her as though she had regained the life she had given up as lost, and she too felt a momentary sense of gratification.

"Won't you come right along in?" said Suezō politely to the old man, motioning toward the room and turning to Otama with an added "Please!" of encouragement. When the two had entered the room, he drew the old woman who had acted as go-between aside, slipped a paper packet into her hand, and whispered something. She bared her discolored teeth in a laugh that was half unctuous, half tinged with contempt and, bobbing her head in acknowledgment, retreated down the corridor.

Suezō returned to the room and, finding his guests crowded in an awkward heap just inside the door, urged them warmly to their places and ordered the dinner from the maid. Presently saké and a few simple appetizers were brought, and as Suezō poured a cup of wine for the father and began to chat with him, he realized that this was not the first time the old man had donned clean clothes and sat in a fine room.

Suezō had at first been irritated at the thought of the father's bothersome presence, but now he began to feel more kindly toward him until at last, contrary to all expectation, the two ended by engaging in convivial conversation. Suezō made every effort to display the best side of his nature, pleased that he should have such an ideal opportunity to instill in the silent, reserved young woman a feeling of confidence in him. By the time the main course was brought in, one might have thought that the group in the little room was a family who, returning from an outing, had dropped in to the restaurant for dinner.

Suezō had all his life been a tyrant to his wife, encountering from her sometimes resistance, at other times passive submission. But now as he gazed at Otama, blushing and smiling while she poured saké for him in place of the maid, he felt a subtle, quiet delight he had never known before. He sat relishing the magical glow of geniality that pervaded the room. But as to why he had never experienced such pleasure in his own home, what might be required to sustain an amiable atmosphere of this kind, or whether his own wife might not be capable of fulfilling the requirements—to questions such as these he gave no careful consideration.

Suddenly from beyond the fence came the sound of wooden clappers and a voice calling, "Here you are! Impersonations of your favorite kabuki actors!" Upstairs the samisen stopped playing and a maid, leaning over the railing, called down a request. "You want Naritaya in the role of Kōchiyama and Otowaya as

Naozamurai? Then that's what you shall have!" said the impersonator as he launched into his performance.

The maid, who had come in with more saké, said, "We're in luck. We have the real impersonator tonight."

Her remark puzzled Suezō. "You mean there are real impersonators and fake impersonators?"

"Yes. Nowadays there's a university student who goes around doing impersonations."

"With musical accompaniment?"

"Oh indeed—costume, musical accompaniment, the whole business. But we can spot him by his voice."

"You mean it's just one person?"

"Yes, there's just one student who does it," said the maid with a laugh.

"Do you know him?"

"Oh yes—he comes here to eat now and then."

"Just think—there are students who can do clever things like that!" Otama's father exclaimed. The maid made no comment.

"Students like that are no good at their studies—you can bet on that!" observed Suezō with a wry smile. He was thinking of the students who came to his place. Some of them were clever at mimicking workmen and amused themselves by strolling around the licensed quarter and joshing with the prostitutes in the smaller houses. Some of them even affected the workmen's manner of speech in their everyday life. But Suezō had not supposed that any student would actually go around doing kabuki impersonations.

He turned to Otama, who had been listening to the conversation in silence. "Who is your favorite actor?"

"I don't have any favorite."

"That's because she's never even seen a kabuki play!" her father chimed in. "We live right behind a kabuki theater and all the young girls in the neighborhood go for a peek. When girls with a taste for that sort of thing hear them tuning up at the theater, they just can't stay at home. But you'll never find Otama among them!"

Before he realized what he was doing, the old man had begun singing his daughter's praises.

Eight

In the end it was decided that Otama would go to live in the Muenzaka house. But the move, which Suezō had imagined would be simple enough, proved to entail a number of complications. Otama asked that a place be found for her father as near to her as possible so she could visit him from time to time and look out for his welfare. It had been her intention from the first to turn over to her father the large part of any allowance she might receive and to hire a young maid so that the old man, now over sixty, would not experience any inconvenience. That way, she reasoned, he need not continue to live in the miserable little house next to the rickshaw shed in Torigoe where they had been up till now, but could move somewhere close by. Thus, just as Suezō had discovered when he intended to arrange a tête-à-tête with Otama that her father must come along too, he now found that in making preparations for his mistress's house he had to make them for the removal of the old man as well.

Of course, since Otama had decided quite on her own that her father should move, she intended to carry out the plan without troubling her patron in any way. But as she discussed the matter with Suezō, he could not very well pretend it was none of his concern. So, impelled by his desire to appear as generous as possible to the young woman who, since their meeting, seemed more desirable than ever, Suezō saw to it that, at the same time Otama moved to Muenzaka, her father should move into the house on the edge of Shinobazu Pond that Suezō had looked at earlier. In discussing plans for him, Otama had indicated that she wanted to pay all the costs involved out of her own allowance. It was obvious to Suezō, however, that that was next to impossible, and he was thus obliged to assist with various and sundry expenditures. The unperturbed air with which he disbursed these funds made the old go-between, who was helping with the arrangements, more than once stare in amazement.

It was the middle of July by the time Otama and her father got moved and settled. Suezō, who pursued his financial affairs with the utmost severity, adopted towards Otama, whose artless speech and behavior had so captured his fancy, the most mild and conciliatory methods, calling each night at Muenzaka to win her affection. As the historians would say, heroes have their gentler side.

Suezō never spent the night, but he came every evening. Through the go-between, he had engaged a young servant girl of thirteen named Ume who romped around the kitchen like a little child playing house. But having no other companion than this to talk to, Otama would by evening begin to feel extremely bored and to long impatiently for Suezō's visit, though she laughed at herself for doing so. When she was living in Torigoe and her father was off at work, leaving her alone to mind the house all day, she would busy herself making the candies that he sold. If I get so many done, she would think, spurring herself on, Papa will surely be surprised when he comes home. So, though she hardly knew any of the other girls in the neighborhood, she had never felt particularly bored. Now, when life had at last become easy for her, she learned for the first time what boredom meant.

But Otama's boredom would be cured when evening came and her patron arrived to keep her company. The case was somewhat different for her father who had moved into the house by the pond. Accustomed to work for a living, he had been thrust so suddenly into a life of ease that at times he felt as though he must be the victim of some conjurer's trick. And those earlier evenings when just he and Otama had sat under the little lamp and talked over the happenings of the day—they were all a beautiful dream, infinitely longed for but now a thing of the past. He never ceased waiting for her, thinking surely she would visit him soon, but day after day went by and Otama never appeared.

For the first day or two, the old man had been so delighted to be in such a beautiful house that he left the maid, a girl from the countryside, to fetch water from the well and tend to the cooking while he busied himself cleaning, putting away his belongings, or sending her to the stores in Nakachō when he discovered some item they needed. Then when evening came, while the maid was clattering around in the kitchen, he would sprinkle water over the area outside the bay window where the Chinese black pine was planted or, puffing on his pipe, would watch the crows raucously circling around the hill at Ueno and the evening haze as it drifted in over the trees of the Benten Shrine and the lotuses blooming on the surface of the pond.

This is fine, one couldn't ask for better! he thought. But from that moment on, he began to have a vague feeling of dissatisfaction, of something missing. It was because Otama, whom he had raised all by himself from the time she was a baby; who understood his thoughts, and he understood hers, even when no words had been spoken; who was kind and considerate in all things and always waited for him when he came home— because Otama was not there. He sat in the window and looked out over the pond. He watched people passing by. That was a big carp that leaped up just now! That Western lady's hat had a whole bird perched on top of it! At such moments he wanted to say, "Otama, look at that!" But she wasn't there—that was what was missing.

By the third or fourth day he began to feel increasingly irritable; it particularly annoyed him when the maid puttered around by his side. It had been many years since he had had a servant of any kind, and being very mild-natured, he was not inclined to scold her. Yet everything she did seemed to conflict with his own way of doing things, and this put him in an irritable mood. No doubt it was because he compared her with Otama, who moved gracefully and went about everything in a quiet, unobtrusive manner. Viewed in such a light the maid, fresh from the country, made a poor showing indeed. Finally on the fourth day, when she brought him his breakfast, she managed to stick her thumb in the *miso* soup as she was handing it to him. "Never mind serving the food!" he said. "Just go in the other room!"

When he had finished breakfast he looked out the window. The sky was cloudy but it did not look like rain; it would probably be cooler and pleasanter than if the weather were clear. He decided to go out, thinking it would help him get over his annoyance at the maid. But he worried that Otama might come while he was away, and as he walked along the edge of the pond, he turned repeatedly to look back at the entrance to his house.

Before long he reached the little bridge where the road leads off from between Kayachō and Shichi-kenchō in the direction of Muenzaka. He thought of dropping by his daughter's house, but that seemed too casual a thing to do. He didn't know just why, but for some reason he hesitated. A mother would probably never stand on ceremony in such fashion, and he wondered again and again why he himself should do so. Yet he did not cross the bridge, but in the end continued walking along the border of the pond.

Suddenly he realized that Suezō's house was right on the other side of the drainage ditch. When he moved into his new house, the old go-between had pointed it out from the window. Looking at it close up, he could see it was very impressive. It was surrounded by a high dirt wall topped with bamboo spikes. The place next door, which he had heard belonged to a famous writer named Fukuchi, had somewhat more spacious grounds, but the house itself was old and lacked the showy, grandiose air that marked Suezō's residence. He stood for a while gazing at the gate of natural wood at the rear entrance, though he felt no desire to see what was inside. Yet he went on standing there blankly, assailed by a kind of indefinable loneliness and desolation. One could perhaps characterize it as the feeling of a father who has come so far down in the world that he has to hand his daughter over to be a mistress.

Soon a whole week had passed and Otama had yet to visit him. He could not help longing for her, but he suppressed such thoughts, pushing them deep down inside him; instead he began speculating whether, now that she was comfortably provided for, she hadn't perhaps forgotten all about her father. To be sure, such conjectures were highly superficial, as though he had deliberately conjured them up merely to have something to occupy his thoughts. Yet he continued to entertain them, though he could never go so far as to be actually angry with his daughter. When speaking to others, we will sometimes say the direct opposite of what we really feel. In just such a way, the old man now tried to tell himself that he would be better off getting angry at her.

Then he started looking at it this way: If I stay in the house all the time I think too much about things. It would be better if I went out. If Otama comes when I'm out, she'll at least think what a waste of time it was to have come all the way over here for nothing. Let that be a lesson to her! With such thoughts in mind, he began going out more.

He would go to Ueno Park, hunt for a bench in a shady spot, and sit down a while. And as he watched the rickshaws, their hoods put up, passing through the park, he would imagine how Otama was perhaps just this moment arriving at his house, and how disconcerted she would be to find him out. He was in a way testing himself to see if he could enjoy the thought of that happening.

Sometimes now he went in the evening to the Fukinukitei Theater to listen to Enchō telling funny stories or to Komanosuke's *gidayū* ballad recitations. And at the theater too he would imagine how she might come to see him when he was out. Or again he would wonder if she wasn't actually in the audience, and would look around to see if he could spot any young women with gingko-leaf hairdos like hers. Once a woman with such a hairdo came in after the intermission, escorted by a man in a summer kimono and a panama hat pulled down over his eyes—panama hats were still a rarity in those days. The pair went to the balcony in the rear of the theater, and when the woman leaned on the railing and peered down at the crowd, the old man thought for just a moment that it really was Otama. But then he noticed that her face was rounder than Otama's and she was shorter in height. Moreover, the man in the panama hat had not only this woman, but three others, in hairdos of various varieties, seated behind him, all geishas or apprentice geishas. "I see we have Mr. Fukuchi with us this evening," remarked a student sitting next to the old man.

When the performance was over and he started home, a woman carrying a long-handled paper lantern with the name Fukinukitei written across it in red appeared to escort the gentleman in the panama and his band of geishas to his home. Till he reached his own home, the old man walked sometimes ahead of them, sometimes in their wake.

Nine

Otama, who had never before been separated from her father, often thought of going to see how he was getting along. She was afraid, however, that Suezō, who came every day, might be annoyed if she were out when he called, and so her plan to visit her father was put off from one day to the next. Suezō never stayed until morning, and often he left as early as eleven. At other times, explaining that he had business that evening, he would stay only long enough for a moment's smoke by the brazier. Yet there was no evening on which Otama could say for sure that he would not come. She might have gone to her father's in the daytime, but Ume, the maid, was such a child that it was impossible to trust her to do anything alone. And in any case, Otama did not care to leave the house when the neighbors could see her. At first she was so shy that she would not venture to the public bath at the foot of the slope without sending the maid down first to see how crowded it was, after which she would slip out to take her bath.

On the third day after moving to the new house, Otama, prone to take fright at almost anything anyway, had an experience that thoroughly shocked her. The day of her arrival, men from the local grocery and fish stores had come with their order books to request her patronage, but on the third day, as the fish man had not called that morning, she sent Ume to the bottom of the hill to buy some fish for lunch.

Otama did not care to eat fresh fish every day; her father, who was not a drinker, had always been satisfied with any sort of simple food, so long as it agreed with him, and she had become accustomed to making do with whatever happened to be in the house. But once in the past a nearby neighbor, by no means prosperous herself, had remarked disparagingly on the fact that Otama and her father went days on end without buying any fresh food. Otama was afraid that Ume might make some similar observation, which would reflect badly on the patron who had been so generous. So she sent the girl to the fish store at the foot of the hill mainly for effect.

But when Ume returned she was in tears. Asked what had happened, this was her reply. She had found the store and gone in, only to discover that it was a different shop from the one that had come to the house to take orders. The proprietor was out and his wife was minding the counter. Probably he had returned from the wholesale fish market, left part of his supply there, and gone off with the rest to make deliveries to customers.

From the heaps of fish laid out on the racks Ume had selected some small mackerel that looked fresh and asked the price. "I don't believe I've seen you before," said the fishwife. "Where do you come from?" Ume described the house on the hill in which she lived, whereupon the woman looked suddenly very cross. "Indeed!" she said. "I'm sorry, then, but you better run along. We have no fish here to sell to a moneylender's mistress!" With this she turned away and went on smoking, not deigning to pay any further attention to the girl.

Ume, too upset to feel like going to any other stores, had come running back, and now, looking very wretched, repeated in disconnected scraps what the fishwife had said.

As Otama listened, her face turned pale and for some time she remained silent. In the heart of the inexperienced young woman a hundred confused emotions mingled chaotically; even she herself could not have untangled their jumbled threads. A great weight pressed down on her heart and the blood from throughout her body rushed to it, leaving her white and cold with perspiration. Her first conscious thought, though surely of no real importance, was that after such an incident Ume would no longer be able to remain in the house.

Ume gazed at the pale, bloodless face of her mistress, sensing merely that she was in great distress without comprehending the cause. She had returned in anger from the store, but she realized that, since there was still nothing for lunch, she could hardly leave things as they were. The money her mistress had given her to do the shopping with was still stuck into the sash of her kimono. "I've never seen such a nasty old woman," she said in an effort to be comforting. "I don't know who would buy her old fish anyway! There's another store down by the Inari Shrine. I'll just run down there and get something, shall I?" Otama felt a momentary joy that Ume had declared herself her ally, and her face reflected a weak smile as she nodded her approval. Ume bounded off with a clatter.

Otama remained for a while without moving. Then her taut nerves began gradually to relax and tears welled up in her eyes. She pulled a handkerchief from her sleeve to press them back. In her mind was only one thought—how dreadful! how dreadful!

Did she hate the fish store for not selling her anything, she wondered, or was she ashamed or sorry that she was the sort of person they would not sell to? No, it was none of these. Nor indeed was it that she hated Suezō, the man to whom she had given herself and who she now knew was a moneylender, nor did she feel any particular shame or regret that she had given herself to such a man. She had heard from others that moneylenders were nasty, frightening people, hated by everyone. But her father had never borrowed money from one. He had always gone to the pawnshop, and even when the clerk there had hardheartedly refused to give him as much as he asked for, the old man never expressed any resentment over the clerk's unreasonableness, but would merely shake his head sadly. As a child fears ghosts or policemen, Otama counted moneylenders among those to be afraid of, but she did so with no very vivid or personal emotion. What then was so dreadful?

In her mortification there was very little hatred for the world or for people. If one were to ask exactly what in fact she resented, one would have to answer that it was her own fate. Through no fault of her own she was made to suffer persecution, and this was what she found so painful. When she was deceived and abandoned by the police officer, she had felt this mortification, and recently, when she realized that she must become a mistress, she experienced it again. Now she learned that she was not only a mistress but the mistress of a despised moneylender, and her despair, which had been ground smooth between the teeth of time and washed of its color in the waters of resignation, assumed once more in her heart its stark outline.

After a while, Otama got up, took from the cupboard a white calico apron that she herself had made and, tying it on, with a deep sigh went into the kitchen. She wore a silk apron only on festive occasions, never when working in the kitchen. Even when she wore a washable summer kimono, she tied a towel around her head so the oil from her hairdo would not soil the collar—so fastidious was she about her clothes.

By this time she had grown quite calm again. Resignation was a mental process she was only too familiar with, and if she directed her mind toward that goal, it operated with the accustomed smoothness of a well-oiled machine.

Ten

One evening Suezō sat by the brazier smoking. From the first evening, whenever Suezō came, Otama would spread a mat for him by the side of the large square brazier, where he would sit at his ease smoking and gossiping. She herself, at a loss to know what to do with her hands, would sit on her side, drumming on the edge of the brazier or playing with the fire tongs, and respond in brief, shy answers. Looking at her, one would suppose that she could not stand to be separated from the brazier, as though it were some sort of rampart she needed to lean on before she could face the enemy.

After they had chatted a while, she would become more voluble, speaking mostly of the minor joys and sorrows she had known during the years with her father. Suezō paid little attention to the content of her remarks but listened rather as to a cricket in a cage whose engaging chirps brought a smile to his face. Then Otama would suddenly become aware of her own garrulousness and, blushing, would break off her story and return to her former silence. All her words and actions were so guileless that to Suezō's ever observant eyes they appeared as transparent as water in a bowl. Sitting with her was for Suezō as pleasant as relaxing in a good bath after a period of strenuous exercise and soaking up its warmth. Her companionship brought a refreshing delight that to him was a totally new experience. In his visits to the house he was subjected to a process of acculturation, like a wild animal learning the ways of human society.

It was three or four days after the incident at the fish store and Suezō was sitting as usual beside the brazier when he began to notice that Otama for no particular reason kept moving restlessly around the room without appearing able to settle down. She had always been slow to answer, her glance shy and evasive, but her behavior tonight had about it a new and unusual air.

"What are you thinking about?" he asked as he filled his pipe.

Otama pulled the drawer at the end of the brazier halfway out and, although there was nothing she was looking for, peered busily into it. "Nothing," she said, turning to him with her large eyes. However it may be in old storybook tales, these were not the kind of eyes that could be trusted to keep a great secret.

Suezō's face unconsciously contracted into a frown, but then as unconsciously brightened again.

"What do you mean, nothing! 'What shall I do, what shall I do?' you're thinking. It's written all over your face," he retorted.

Otama flushed and for a moment remained silent while she considered what to say. The workings of the delicate apparatus of her mind became almost visible. "I've been thinking for a long time that I ought to go visit my father," she said. Tiny insects that must forever be escaping from the pursuit of more powerful creatures have their protective coloring; women tell lies.

Suezō laughed and spoke in a scolding voice. "What? Your father living by the pond right in front of your nose and you haven't been to see him yet? He's hardly any farther than the Iwasaki mansion across the way, practically in the same house with you. You can go now if you like. Or better still, tomorrow morning."

Otama, twirling the ashes with the fire tongs, stole a glance at Suezō. "I was just wondering whether it would be all right—"

"Oh, come now, there's no need to wonder about a thing like that! How long will you stay a child?" This time his voice was gentle.

And there the matter ended, for Suezō went so far as to say that if she found it bothersome to go alone, he would come in the morning and go with her the four or five blocks to her father's house.

Otama had been wondering several things lately. She wondered why her patron, who when he was with her always seemed so trustworthy, so thoughtful and gentle, should engage in such a hateful occupation. It seemed strange, and she wondered, if she spoke to him about it, whether she could not persuade him to go into a more respectable line of business. But though she entertained unreasonable speculations of this type, she never thought of him as in any way a disagreeable person.

Suezō for his part was vaguely aware that there was something on Otama's mind that she was hiding, but when he tried to discover what it was, she replied like a child that it was nothing. Still, as he left the house sometime after eleven and walked slowly down the slope of Muenzaka, he knew there was something there. And with his usual keen powers of observation he perceived that the matter could not be ignored. Someone had told her something that had suddenly aroused in her a feeling of uneasiness; that much he could guess. But what she had heard, or from whom, he could not tell.

Eleven

When Otama arrived at her father's house by the pond in Ikenohata the next morning, he had just finished breakfast. Otama, who had hurried out without even taking time to put on makeup, wondered if she would be too early, but the old man, accustomed to early rising, had already swept the entranceway and sprinkled water around to settle the dust. Then, after washing up and seating himself on the new tatami mats, he had eaten his usual lonely morning meal.

Two or three houses away, an inn where geishas entertained had opened recently and it was sometimes noisy in the evening. But the houses on either side of her father's place had their lattice doors still shut, and in the early morning the surroundings seemed unusually quiet. From the bay window of her father's house one could see, through the branches of the Chinese black pine, the willow limbs swaying slightly in the fresh breeze, and beyond, the lotus leaves that covered the surface of the pond. Here and there among their green shone the pink dots of blossoms newly opened in the morning sun. The house, which faced north, would perhaps be rather cold in winter, but in summer it was ideal.

Since Otama had been old enough to think for herself she had considered how, should fortune ever come her way, she would do this or that for her father, and now as she saw before her eyes the house she had provided for him, the fulfillment of her long-cherished hopes, she could not help feeling joyful. In her joy, however, was mingled a drop of bitterness. If it were not for that, how great her happiness would be at meeting her father today. But, as she thought with irritation, one can't have the world just as one would like it.

There had as yet been no visitors to the house, and when the old man heard the sound of someone at the gate, he put down the cup of tea he was drinking and glanced in surprise toward the entrance hall. While she was still hidden by the double-leaf screen in the hall, he heard Otama's voice call "Papa!" Restraining his impulse to jump up in greeting, he sat where he was and debated what to say to her. "It was so good of you to remember your old father," he thought of saying in spite, but when his beloved daughter suddenly appeared by his side, he could not get out the words. Disgruntled as he was, he only gazed in silence at her face.

How lovely she was! He had always taken pride in her, and even in the midst of poverty had tried to spare her hardship and to see that she was neatly dressed. But in the ten days since he had seen her last, she seemed to have become a totally different person. No matter how busy she was, she instinctively kept herself clean and neat. But the daughter he remembered from past days was an unpolished gem compared to the carefully groomed woman he now faced. Whether a father perceives it in a daughter or an older man in a young woman, beauty is beauty. And beauty has the power to melt the heart; no father, no older man can resist it. Otama's father had intended to look very stern, but somehow against his will his expression softened.

Otama, thrust into a wholly new environment and separated from her father for the first time, had thought only of how much she wanted to see him again. Yet she had let some ten days go by without doing so. She had come with many things to say, but as she looked at him delightedly she could for the moment find no words to express them.

"Shall I take the tray away?" asked the maid in her country dialect, poking her head in from the kitchen. Otama, unaccustomed to her way of speaking, did not catch the words. The maid, her hair rolled up on a comb in a manner that made her head seem too small for the plump face, stared rudely at Otama in her surprise.

"Yes, take it away and bring some fresh tea. Use the green tea on the shelf," said the old man, pushing the tray away from him. The maid carried it into the kitchen.

"Oh, please don't bother to make special tea!" Otama protested.

"Nonsense! I have some crackers here too." The old man rose and brought some egg crackers from a tin in the cupboard, arranging them in a cake dish. "They make these right back of the Hōtan Pharmacy. This is a very convenient neighborhood for shopping. In the alley near there I can buy Jōen's soy sauce relish."

"Jōen! I remember when you took me to the Yanagihara Theater to hear Jōen tell his stories. That time it was something about a banquet he went to and how good everything tasted, and he said, 'It tasted almost as good as the soy sauce relish I make in my store!' Didn't the audience laugh! Such a fat, jolly man, and when he came on stage and suddenly flipped up the rear of his kimono before he sat down—it struck me as so funny! You should get fat like that, Papa."

"I couldn't stand being that fat," said the old man as he put the dish of crackers down by his daughter.

Soon tea was brought and the two chatted without pause as if they had never been apart. Then the old man suddenly asked in a rather embarrassed tone, "How are things? Does your master come to see you sometimes?"

"Yes," said Otama, and for a moment she seemed unable to answer more. It was not "sometimes" that Suezō came, but every evening without fail. Had she just been married and been asked if she was getting along well with her husband, she might have replied with great cheerfulness that she was doing extremely well. But in her present position the fact that Suezō came every night seemed almost shameful, and she found it difficult to mention. She thought for a moment and then replied, "Things seem to be going all right, Papa. There's nothing for you to worry about."

"Well, that's good," he said, though he felt a certain lack of assurance in his daughter's answer. An evasiveness had come into their speech. The two, who up until now had always spoken with complete freedom, who had never had the slightest secret from one another, found themselves forced against their will to address each other like strangers and to maintain a certain reserve. In the past, when they had been deceived by the fraudulent police officer, they had been ashamed before the neighbors, but both of them had known in their hearts that the blame lay with him, and they had discussed the whole terrible affair without the slightest reserve. But now, when their plans had turned out successfully and they were comfortably established, a new shadow, an air of sadness, hovered over their conversation.

The old man was anxious to have a more concrete answer. "What sort of man is he?" he began again.

"Well—" said Otama thoughtfully, inclining her head to one side and speaking as though to herself, "I surely don't think he is a *bad* person. We haven't been together very long, but so far he has never used any harsh language or anything like that."

"Oh?" said the old man with a look of dissatisfaction. "And is there any reason to suppose that he *is* a bad person?"

Otama looked quickly at her father and her heart began to pound. If she was to say what she had come to say, now was the time to say it. But the thought of inflicting a new blow on her father, now that she had at last brought him peace of mind, was too painful. She resolved to go away without revealing her secret, and at the crucial moment she turned the conversation in another direction.

"They said he was a man who had done all sorts of things to build up a fortune for himself. I didn't know what to expect, and I was rather worried. But he's— well, what would you say—chivalrous. Whether that's his real nature I can't say, but he is certainly making an effort to act that way. As long as he tries to be chivalrous, that's enough, don't you think, Papa?" She looked up at her father. For a woman, no matter how honest, to hide what is in her heart and talk of something else is not so difficult as it is for a man. It is possible that in such a situation the more volubly she speaks, the more honest she really is.

"Perhaps you are right. But somehow you speak as though you don't trust the man," her father said.

Otama smiled. "I've grown up, Papa. From now on I don't intend to be made a fool of by others. I intend to be strong."

The old man, suddenly sensing that his daughter, usually so mild and submissive, was for once turning the point of her remarks at him, looked at her uneasily. "Well, it's true, as you know, that I've gone through life pretty consistently being made a fool of. But you will feel a good deal better in your heart if you are cheated by others than if you are always doing the cheating. Whatever business you are in, you must never be dishonest, and you must remember those who have been kind to you."

"Don't worry. You always used to say that I was an honest child, and I still am. But I've been thinking quite a bit lately. I want no more of being taken in by people."

"You mean you don't trust what your master says?"

"Yes, that's it. He thinks I'm just a child. Compared to him, perhaps I am, but I'm not as much a child as he thinks."

"Has he told you anything that you've discovered to be untrue?"

"Indeed he has! You remember how the old go-between kept saying that his wife had died and left him with the children, and that if I accepted his proposal it would be just as though I were a proper wife? She told us that it was just to keep up appearances that he couldn't let me live in his own home. Well, it so happens that he *has* a wife. He said so himself, just like that. I was so surprised I didn't know what to do."

The father's eyes widened. "So the go-between was just trying to make it sound like a good match—"

"Of course, he has to keep everything about me a strict secret from his wife," Otama continued. "He tells her all kinds of lies, so I hardly expect him to speak nothing but the truth to me. I intend to take anything he says with a grain of salt."

The old man sat holding the burnt-out pipe he had been smoking and looked blankly at his daughter. She seemed suddenly to have grown so much older and more serious. "I must be getting back," she said hurriedly, as though she had just remembered something. "Now that I've seen that everything is all right, I'll be visiting you every day. I had hesitated because I thought I'd better get his permission first, but last night he finally told me I could come. Now I have to run. The maid is such a child she can't even fix lunch unless I'm there to help."

"If you got permission from him to come, why don't you eat lunch here?" the old man asked.

"No, I don't think I'd better. I'll come again very soon, Papa. Good-bye!"

As Otama got up to leave, the maid hurried to the entrance hall to arrange her wooden clogs for her. A bit dull-witted, the maid was still a woman, and as such felt compelled to scrutinize any other woman she encountered. A philosopher assures us that women regard all other women as rivals, even the unknown ones they pass on the street. Clumsy and countrified as the maid was, sticking her thumb in the soup, she could hardly ignore someone as beautiful as Otama, and had probably been listening in on the conversation between Otama and her father.

"Come again when you can," said the old man without rising, "and give my kindest regards to your master."

Otama pulled a little purse from her black satin sash, took out some money and, wrapping it in paper, gave it to the maid. Then she slipped into her clogs and went out the lattice door.

She had come intending to bare the bitterness in her heart and share her misfortune with her father, but to her own surprise she now found herself leaving almost in good spirits. She had decided not to inflict further worry on her father now that he was at ease, but rather to show him how strong and trustworthy she could be. As she endeavored to convey this in her conversation, she became aware of a kind of awakening within herself. She, who in the past had depended so much on others, now experienced a surprising sense of independence. Her face was cheerful as she walked along the edge of the pond.

Although the sun, now risen high above Ueno Hill, beat down fiercely, making the vermilion pillars of the Benten Shrine redder than ever, Otama carried her little foreign-style parasol in her hand without troubling to put it up.

Twelve

One night Suezō returned from Muenzaka to find that his wife, Otsune, had put the children to bed but was still up herself. Generally when she put the children to bed she lay down on her pallet beside them. Tonight, however, she sat staring at the floor and, though well aware when Suezō crawled in under the mosquito net, made no move to look up.

Suezō's pallet was laid far over by the wall, separated a little from the other pallets. By the pillow was a mat, along with his smoking tray and tea things. He sat down, lit a cigarette, and asked in a gentle voice, "What's the matter? You're not asleep yet?"

Otsune was silent. Suezō decided to give in no further. He had made the peace overture, and if she did not respond, he would leave it at that. He smoked his cigarette with a deliberate air of unconcern.

"Where have you been till now?" she asked, suddenly raising her head and looking at him. Since they had begun to employ servants, the couple had made an effort to speak in a more refined manner; but when they were alone, they reverted to their former rough language. In Otsune's question, only the polite pronoun *anata* remained.

Suezō looked at his wife sharply but made no reply. She was aware of something, he realized, but since he could not judge the extent of her knowledge, he would remain silent. He was not one to provide his opponent with ammunition by blurting out anything.

"I know all about it!" she shrilled, tears choking her voice.

"What do you mean? What do you know all about?" His voice was soft and compassionate and he spoke as though in utter surprise.

"The nerve! Sitting there as though you don't know what I mean!" His complacency only nettled her. Her voice broke and she dabbed at her tears with the sleeve of her nightgown.

"If you talk like that, I don't know what I'm supposed to say," he replied.

"What's that? I ask you where you've been this evening and you sit there pretending! Telling me you have business to tend to and all the time you're keeping some woman—" Her flat-nosed face was red from tears, and the locks of tangled hair clung to it in globs. Her little moist eyes glared at him as she crawled quickly to his side and clutched with all her might at the hand that held the cigarette.

"Stop it!" he said, shaking his hand free and beating out the sparks that had scattered over the straw matting. She seized his hand again and spoke through her sobs. "What kind of man are you? You manage to make a little money and then you go around like a lord and won't even buy your wife so much as a new kimono. Leave me here to look after the children while you go running after some woman!"

"Stop it, I said!" He spoke in a low, fierce voice, shaking her off again. "Do you want to wake the children? They can hear you all the way to the maid's room!"

The youngest child rolled over and mumbled in its sleep. Otsune thrust her face close to Suezō's chest and, sobbing uncontrollably now, spoke in a low voice. "Just what am I supposed to do?"

"You don't have to do anything," he said. "You're too good-hearted a person and you've let someone take you in. Who's been telling you about kept women?" Suezō gazed at her *marumage* hairdo, disheveled now and shaken with sobs, the hairdo of a married woman, and wondered why it was always so unbecoming on a homely woman. And as her sobbing subsided, he shifted his gaze to the big breasts, hanging down to her stomach, that had fed his children so well, and repeated the question. "Who told you that?"

"It doesn't matter who told me, because it's true!" He could feel the breasts pressing against him.

"It is *not* true and it *does* matter. Tell me who said it!" he demanded.

74.

"All right, I don't care. It was the lady at the Uokin."

"I can't understand anything you say if you don't speak up—mumble-mumble, mumble-mumble."

Otsune lifted her head and gave a laugh of disgust. "The lady at the Uokin fish store! Isn't that what I said?"

"Oh, her! I thought it must be somebody like that." Suezō looked gently at the upturned face of his wife and lit another cigarette. "The papers are always talking about the 'arbiters of society,' though I don't believe I've ever seen one. Maybe they mean scandal-mongers like that old fishwife. We've got a lot of busybodies in this neighborhood. You certainly don't expect to take what they say as the truth, I hope. Now listen carefully and I'll tell you the truth."

Otsune sat silent and expressionless, as though enveloped in a fog, her only emotion one of deep suspicion that she was being tricked. She looked attentively at her husband, listening carefully to what he was saying. It was Suezō's habit at such times to use difficult expressions like "arbiters of society" that he had picked up from the newspapers so that the poor woman, unable to follow his argument, would in the end timidly acquiesce.

"You remember that Mr. Yoshida who used to come to the house when I was still at the university?"

Suezō went on, puffing on his cigarette. "The man with the gold-rimmed glasses and fancy silk clothes? He's at some hospital in Chiba now, but he still hasn't settled his account with me, though it's been two or three years. From the time he was living in the dormitory, he's been tied up with some woman. Till recently she was running a little rented store in Nanamagari. He used to send her an allowance every month, but this year she hasn't had even a letter from him, much less any money. She asked me to contact him and see if I couldn't find out what's wrong. When Yoshida wanted his note renewed, he was afraid to come to my place because people might see him, so he used to ask me to go to her store to make the transaction. That's how she happened to know me.

"It was a lot of bother, but since I was after him about my own account anyway, I tried to do what I could for the woman. Things still aren't settled, and she keeps pestering me with her troubles. In addition, she asked if I knew of a nice cheap place she could move to, so I found her a little house up by Kiridōshi that belonged to the parents of a pawnbroker. She just moved in, and sometimes I drop by for a smoke or two. I suppose some fool in the neighborhood has been inventing stories about us. Next door is a sewing teacher with a lot of girls and they like to gab. I can't imagine what man would be fool enough to try to keep a mistress in that neighborhood!" He ended with a scornful laugh.

Otsune had been listening intently, her little eyes aglow. Now she spoke in a milder tone. "Maybe it's the way you say. But I don't know what may happen if you keep going to a place like that. After all, she's a woman who can be had for money—"

"Nonsense! I have you. Why would I play around with anyone else? Have I ever done anything like that in the past? We're too old for jealous quarrels. Let's not do this anymore." Confident of the easy success of his explanation, Suezō was already savoring his triumph.

"But you're the kind of person women all take a fancy to, and I worry about it," she protested.

"Oh, come now, you're just prejudiced. Who besides you would put up with someone like me? It's after one. Let's get some sleep."

Thirteen

The pastiche of truth and fabrication that Suezō offered by way of explanation for a time cooled his wife's jealousy. But it was no more than a temporary palliative, for as long as the woman on Muenzaka remained as before, there was to be no end to the gossip and grumbling. The maid, for example, would report to Otsune that "So-and-so saw the master today going in the lattice door!"

Suezō made excuses. "Business!" he would say, and when Otsune objected that he could have no business to attend to at night, he would reply, "And who is going to talk about borrowing money early in the morning?" If she asked why he had never been this busy in the past, he would explain that he was operating on a grander scale now.

Until Suezō moved to the house by the pond, he had handled all his moneylending affairs personally. But now he not only had set up a kind of office near his house, but also had taken a house in Ryūsenjimachi that functioned as a branch office. Thus students desiring to borrow money need not go a long way to do so. Those in Nezu could go to the office near Suezō's house, those in Yoshiwara could go to the branch office. Later he made arrangements with a teahouse called Nishinomiya in the Yoshiwara prostitute quarter to act as an outlet for his branch office. Hence, if a person was known at the branch office, he could disport himself at the teahouse without having to pay cash. In effect, Suezō acted as a kind of commissariat for frequenters of the pleasure quarter.

Suezō and his wife continued for a month without further friction; so long was Suezō's sophistry effective. It was from an unexpected direction one morning that a new discord arose.

Informing her husband, who happened to be home, that she was going shopping while the morning was still cool, Otsune left the house with the maid and walked to Hirokōji. On their way home, as they passed through Nakachō, the maid suddenly pulled at Otsune's sleeve.

"What is it?" Otsune asked crossly, looking around. The girl pointed to a woman standing in front of a shop on the left. Otsune grudgingly looked in that direction, unconsciously slowing her steps, and at that instant the woman in front of the shop turned around. The two women stared at one another.

Otsune thought at first that she was a geisha. If so, on the basis of her momentary glimpse she supposed there must be few even in Sukiyamachi as striking as this one. But in the next instant she realized that the woman lacked something that a geisha would surely possess. It was a certain extravagance of attitude. A geisha will wear her clothes beautifully, but there is an overstatement in the beauty that rules out modesty. What this woman lacked was precisely that touch of overstatement.

The woman in front of the store, aware that someone had stopped to look at her, glanced around. But finding nothing of note in the person who eyed her, she placed her parasol between her knees and bent forward to peer into the little purse she had taken from her sash. She was searching for a coin.

The store, on the south side of Nakachō, was the Tashigaraya, a name that inspired some wag to observe that "Tashigaraya read backwards means 'We did it!'" The shop with this odd name sold toothpowder in red packets with gold lettering. At that time foreign toothpaste had not yet been imported, and the only toothpowders that were of good quality and not gritty were the peony-scented Kaōsan sold at the Kishida and that sold at the Tashigaraya. Otama had stopped to buy a packet of the latter on the way back from her early morning visit to her father.

When Otsune had gone on a few steps, the maid whispered, "That's her. The woman from Muenzaka!" As Otsune nodded in silence, the maid wondered why her words had produced no greater effect. But at the same moment Otsune decided that the figure in front of the shop was not a geisha, she had instinctively recognized her as the woman from Muenzaka. She had been aided in her conclusion by the assumption that the maid had not pointed her out merely for her beauty, but another factor added its weight. It was the parasol that Otama rested between her knees.

A month or so earlier, when Suezō had gone to Yokohama, he had brought back a foreign-style parasol as a present for his wife. The handle was very long and in proportion made the top seem too small. Twirled playfully in the hands of a tall Western lady it might have been charming, but on the squat, chubby Otsune it resembled nothing so much as a child's diaper stuck on the end of a laundry pole. She had never used it. It was covered in white cloth dyed with blue checks and was exactly the same, Otsune realized, as the parasol carried by the woman in front of the Tashigaraya.

As they turned the corner by the saké shop and started toward the pond, the maid tried to cheer her mistress up. "I don't think she's so pretty at all, do you? Her face is too flat and she's so awfully tall!"

"We can do without comment from you!" said Otsune, refusing to join in the game, and quickened her steps. Rebuffed in her effort, the maid trailed after her with an injured look.

Everything was turmoil in Otsune's mind; she could think of nothing clearly. Without having any idea what she would say to her husband, she felt she must confront him at once, must say something. When he bought me that parasol, how happy I was, she thought. He had never bought me anything before unless I asked him. I wondered why he would do such a strange thing, why he was suddenly so kind. Now I know. *She* asked him to buy her one, and so he got one for me too. Exactly! And I thanked him so, when I can't even use it!

Not only the parasol, but her kimono and hair ornaments—I'll bet he bought all of them. Everything she's wearing is as different from what I'm wearing as this sateen sunshade I'm carrying is from that imported parasol. And then when I ask for some new clothes for the children he won't even give me the money. Says the boy can make do with one suit of clothes, or that it's just a waste of money to make kimonos for a little girl. Did anyone ever hear of the wife and children of a man as rich as he is going around dressed the way we are? And it's all because of that woman that he treats us like this!

He says she's Yoshida's woman, but who's going to believe that? He's most likely been keeping her from the time she was in the Nanamagari store. That's it! After he made a little money and started getting extravagant with his clothes, he said it was all for business appearances, but it was because of her. He wouldn't take me anywhere, but you can be sure he was taking her places. To think of it!—

"Where are you going, ma'am?" the maid suddenly called to her. Staring at the ground and hurrying along, Otsune had gone past the gate of her own house. The maid laughed out loud.

Fourteen

When Otsune, having cleared away the breakfast things, went out shopping in the early morning, she had left Suezō smoking and reading the newspaper. But when she returned, she found him gone. She had come home determined that, if he was still there, she would thrash things out with him. She wasn't sure just what she would say, but she fully intended to face up to him this time and speak out. His absence thus left her feeling flat.

But there was lunch to prepare, and the lined kimonos that the children would soon be needing for the cooler weather. And as she went about these activities in a mechanical manner, the fury with which she had meant to confront her husband gradually abated. More than once in the past she had rushed at him, determined if need be to dash her head against the stone wall of his resistance, only to find to her surprise that he offered little or no resistance at all. Instead he would begin in his glib way expounding on the whys and wherefores of the situation until, though not really convinced by his reasons, she would find herself somehow talked into meek submission. And she was not at all sure that the attack she had planned to launch today would fare any better than had those earlier ones.

Otsune ate lunch with the children, intervened in their squabbles, stitched together their fall kimonos, and got their supper ready. Pouring water in a tin tub, she gave them a simple bath and took one herself. Then, lighting a smudge coil to keep off the mosquitoes, she ate supper with them. When they returned from their after-supper play, the maid, finished in the kitchen, spread the sleeping mats in the usual places and put up the mosquito net, after which Otsune, having supervised a final washup, put the children to bed. Then she arranged her husband's supper on a tray, covered it with a net to keep off the flies, and, putting a kettle on the charcoal brazier so he would have hot water, placed these things in the next room. This was what she always did when he was late coming home.

Having carried out these chores in her mechanical manner, Otsune picked up a fan and seated herself in the middle of the mosquito net. That woman I saw this morning—right now he's at her place! she thought. She could picture it clearly. She couldn't go on just sitting there—what should she do? What should she do? She felt like dashing off to the house on Muenzaka and having a look for herself.

Once, when she was on her way to Fujimura to buy some of the bean cakes that the children were so fond of, she had gone by Muenzaka and had looked at the house next to the sewing teacher's, thinking, This must be it, the one with the lattice door! She would just go now and have a look at it. Perhaps she could see a light shining from it, or perhaps catch the faint sound of voices. Even that would be enough.

But no, she thought, I couldn't do that. I couldn't leave the house without going down the corridor past the maid's room. This time of year the sliding doors will be open and Matsu will surely be sitting up sewing. If she asks where I'm going, what will I say? If I say I'm going to buy something, Matsu will insist on going herself. As much as I'd like to slip out and have a look, it just isn't possible.

Well then, what should I do? When I came home this morning, I wanted to have it out with him as soon as possible. But suppose he had been here—what would I have said? Whatever I said, he would have come out with some vague, incomprehensible answer, the way he always does. And he would twist things around and in the end make a fool of me. He's too clever a talker—whenever we argue, I always lose. Should I just keep quiet then? But if I do, what will happen? As long as that woman is around, he doesn't care what becomes of me! What should I do? What should I do?

These were the thoughts that went round and round in her mind, and always they returned to the same starting point. Before long her head felt so muddled she could no longer think at all. She was certain of only one thing: that it would be useless to resort to violent argument with her husband. That she must avoid.

At that point Suezō came into the room. Otsune fiddled with the handle of her fan as though it had suddenly become of great interest to her.

"What's this—acting strange again? What's the matter?" The fact that his wife had not bothered to give her customary greeting did not seem to anger him. He was in a good mood.

Otsune remained silent. She had hoped to avoid an argument, but now that her husband had come home, her anger and resentment came welling up and she felt she must make some sort of protest.

"Some silly idea on your mind again? Forget it! Forget it!" Suezō put his hand on his wife's shoulder, gave her two or three gentle shakes, and then sat down on his own sleeping mat.

"I was just wondering what I ought to do. I should go home, I suppose, but I have no home to go to. And then there are the children—"

"What do you mean, what should you do? You don't have to do anything. Thing's are fine just as they are. All's right with the world, as they say."

"Yes. All's right as far as you're concerned because you don't care what happens to me."

"What a funny thing to say! What's going to happen to you? Nothing's going to happen. Just go on the way you are."

"That's right—make fun of me! You don't care whether I'm around or not, and that's why you never listen seriously to anything I say. No, I've got it wrong. Actually, I'm sure you'd much rather I *weren't* around!"

"That's an outlandish thing to say—that I'd rather you weren't around! If you weren't around, I'd be in a fix, wouldn't I? For one thing, I depend on you to look after the children. And that's a big job!"

"Later, though, a beautiful mother will come to look after them. But of course then they'll be stepchildren."

"What do you mean? With both of us right here, how could they be stepchildren?"

"They will, though. I'm sure. But you never think of anyone but yourself! Do you mean to let things go on like this?"

"Of course—why not?"

"With the beautiful lady and the ugly old woman sporting identical parasols?"

"What? What's all this? Sounds like something out of a comedy routine!"

"Of course. I'm never allowed to play a serious part!"

"Now let's stop the fooling and talk reasonably. What's this about parasols?"

"As though you didn't know!"

"Know what? I haven't the faintest idea what you mean!"

"Then I'll refresh your memory. Some time ago you brought me a parasol you bought in Yokohama."

"So I did. What about it?"

"But it wasn't just me you bought one for."

"It wasn't? Then who else would I get one for?"

"I know. You bought one for that woman on Muenzaka, and while you were at it you thought you'd buy me one too." Otsune had brought up the subject of the parasol, but now, as she came to the crux of the affair, she felt her earlier rage and resentment boiling up again.

Suezō, wincing at the accuracy of her attack, was almost tempted to reply, "You hit it!" But instead he assumed a dumbfounded air. "Of all the nonsense! You mean to say that Yoshida's woman has the same kind of parasol as the one I bought you?"

"Because you bought them both. So of course we've both got the same kind!" Otsune's voice took on a shriller tone.

"Oh, this is too silly! Please, now. When I bought the parasol in Yokohama, I remember the man said it was a sample that had just come in. So by now the same article must be on sale anywhere on the Ginza. And because of that I get unjustly accused, like some poor fellow in a play! I take it you ran into Yoshida's woman somewhere. But how did you know her?"

"Oh, I knew her all right. Everyone around here does. Because she's such a 'beauty!'" said Otsune, her voice full of spite. In the past she had in the end let herself be persuaded by Suezō's evasions and excuses. But this time her perception of the situation was too vivid; the facts seemed to lie right before her eyes. Under no circumstances could she accept Suezō's version of the affair.

Suezō, wondering how the two women had met and whether they had exchanged any words, sensed that it would not be to his advantage to probe for details. He thus deliberately refrained from further inquiry. "Beauty? You call her a beauty? A woman with a face as flat as that?"

Otsune remained silent. But the fact that her husband had commented so unfavorably on the face of the woman she hated went some way to placate her feelings.

That evening, after engaging in this heated exchange, the couple managed to reach a kind of reconciliation. But in Otsune's heart a rankling remained, like the pain of an unremoved thorn.

Fifteen

The atmosphere at Suezō's house settled into a ponderous gloom. Sometimes Otsune did nothing but stare blankly into the air, neglecting the children completely. When they came to ask her for something, she would instantly start scolding them vehemently. After she had scolded them she would suddenly realize what she had done and apologize or sit weeping alone. If the maid inquired what to prepare for supper, Otsune would make no reply, or say, "Fix anything you like."

Although Suezō's children were ostracized by their classmates at school because of their father's profession, Suezō, fastidious as he was, had always had his wife dress and keep them spotlessly clean. But now they went about their play with dirty heads and kimonos that were coming apart at the seams. The maid grumbled about Otsune's behavior, but, as a horse will stop to eat grass by the wayside when it knows it has an unskilled rider, she herself grew slipshod in her ways, until the fish rotted in the pantry and the vegetables shriveled and dried up.

Suezō, who liked everything in his home neat and methodical, could not help feeling pained by this disorder. But as he realized it was his own fault, he could hardly complain. It had always been his custom when reproving others to do so in a light, jesting manner that was intended to make the other party reflect on his or her own failings, but this laughing air of his now seemed only to aggravate Otsune's irritation.

Observing his wife in silence, Suezō discovered a curious fact. While he was around the house, she acted very strangely, but when he was away she seemed to come to her senses and go about her work as usual. Having confirmed this observation by questioning the children and the maid, he was at first puzzled. With his usual shrewdness he pondered the situation. His behavior greatly angered his wife, and as long as he was in her presence, the sickness possessed her. He had hoped to avoid giving her the impression that he had grown cold or that there was any estrangement between them. But if, on the contrary, his being around the house merely irritated her, then what he had intended as a cure was in fact making the sickness worse. That clearly would not do. In the future, Suezō decided, he would try the opposite approach.

Accordingly, Suezō began leaving the house earlier than usual and returning later at night. This proved to have a very poor effect. At first his wife only observed his early departures in startled silence. But when he returned late at night she was no longer able to maintain her pouting, negative attitude but flew at him, her patience exhausted. "Where have you been until now?" she demanded, bursting into torrents of tears.

The next time he tried to leave early in the morning, she insisted he tell her where he was going. When he told her, she replied, "You're lying!" She pleaded with him to wait, saying she had something important to ask, clung to his sleeve, blocked his way in the entrance hall and, heedless of the eyes of the maid, did everything she could to detain him.

Unpleasantness of this sort Suezō customarily treated in a jocular manner so as not to make matters worse, but there were times now when in full view of the maid he roughly shook himself free from his wife's frantic grapplings and she fell to the floor. If at such times Suezō agreed to put off his departure and inquired what it was she wanted to ask, she would demand to know, "What do you intend to do about me? What is to become of me if you keep on this way?"—difficult questions that could hardly be settled in a morning. In effect, Suezō's scheme of remedying his wife's sickness by leaving the house early and returning late proved to be totally ineffective.

Suezō considered once more. While he was in the house, his wife was at her worst. But if he made a move to leave, she attempted to stop him. She was deliberately trying to hold him by her side, trying to keep herself upset. And in that connection Suezō remembered something.

When the medical school was still in Shitaya there was a student named Ikai to whom Suezō had lent money. Ikai affected to give no thought to his personal appearance, but went around with bare feet stuck into a pair of tall wooden clogs, his left shoulder hunched up two or three inches above the right one. He was unable to repay the money he had borrowed, but instead of renewing the note, attempted to dodge Suezō entirely. One day, however, Suezō happened to run into him on a street corner in Aoishi Yokochō. When Suezō asked where he was going, Ikai replied that he was off to his jujitsu teacher's house nearby. He added that he would be repaying the loan soon and then slipped away.

Suezō pretended to go on his way, but instead returned surreptitiously to the street corner and looked to see where Ikai had gone. He had gone into the Iyomon Restaurant. Having determined this, Suezō tended to the business in Hirokōji that had brought him to the neighborhood and then, a little while later, strolled into the Iyomon.

Ikai was understandably startled, but with the bravado that seemed inherent in his nature, he insisted that Suezō join his lively party, which consisted of Ikai and two geishas he had summoned. "No excuses, now!" he said. "Today you must keep me company in a drink!"

He was determined that Suezō join the group. That was Suezō's first experience drinking with geishas. One of them was a strikingly chic woman named Oshun. When she had had quite a lot to drink, she sat down in front of Ikai, evidently peeved about something, and began berating him. Suezō listened in silence, but her words stuck in his memory. "Mr. Ikai, you put on a gruff appearance, but in fact you haven't an ounce of spunk in you! I'll just tell you something. No woman will ever care anything for a man who doesn't knock her around once in a while. Keep that in mind!"

Perhaps that was true, thought Suezō, not just of geishas but of any kind of woman. Nowadays Otsune was always dragging him to her side, her face puffed out, arguing and contradicting, as though she wanted him to do something. She wanted him to hit her, that was it! There was no other explanation.

In the past he had worked her like an ox or a horse, till she ceased to be a woman and had turned into a sort of beast. Now suddenly they had a nice house and a maid and she was called "Madam" and lived like a human being, so that she had become like other women again. As Oshun had said, she wanted to be knocked around.

So long as he got their money, Suezō thought, he never cared what people said to him. He had made up to little students still wet behind the ears, following them around, bowing and calling them "Sir." He had gone through life being kicked and stepped on. But nothing mattered as long as he did not lose out in the end.

Day after day, wherever he went, whoever he was dealing with, he cringed and groveled his way along. But observing the general run of men, he noticed that those who bowed and scraped before their superiors would turn around and bully those who were under them, abusing anyone weaker than themselves, getting drunk and beating their wives and children. As far as Suezō was concerned, however, there were no superiors or inferiors. He would bow down to anyone he could get money out of. For the rest, it was all the same to him whether they came or went. They were no concern of his. You would never find him going to all the trouble of knocking people around. If he had that much leisure to spare, he would spend it toting up his interest. That went for the way he treated his wife as well.

Otsune wanted him to play rough with her? Well, that was too bad, but she would never get that kind of treatment. Not from him! He didn't mind squeezing every drop he could get out of anyone who owed him money. But as for knocking people around—that was beyond him. Such were Suezō's thoughts on the matter.

Sixteen

The flow of people up and down Muenzaka increased markedly. It was September, classes at the university had begun, and the students, home for the summer, now hurried back to their lodgings in the Hongō area.

Although the mornings and evenings were cool, the midday sun still shone hot. At Otama's house the bamboo blinds, newly installed when she moved in, had not had time to fade from their initial green, having hung just inside the lattice of the bay window, shielding it from top to bottom. Otama, perishing of boredom, sat in the window, leaning against the pillar with its holder of round painted fans, and stared absently through the blinds at the passersby.

From about three in the afternoon, groups of three or four students would stroll by. On each such occasion, the sparrowlike chatter of the girls in the sewing teacher's house next door would rise to a new pitch of shrillness. Wondering what had inspired the latest outburst, Otama would fix her attention more closely on the figures in the street.

At this time the majority of the students affected the brash, swaggering air that later came to be known as "the hero's pose." A rare few had the look of real gentlemen, invariably students just about to graduate. Those with pale, delicately molded features failed to elicit a favorable response because of their shallow, conceited manner. Others appeared to be too rough to appeal to a woman's eye, though some among these were perhaps excellent scholars. Whatever the type, Otama, without really meaning to, would each day watch them pass by her window. And then one day she became aware of something that startled her, something that seemed to have sprouted in her mind. Engendered in the realm below the threshold of consciousness, it suddenly burst upon her in the form of crowded imaginings that filled her with alarm.

With no other objective than to insure the comfort and happiness of her father, Otama had argued away the objections of the straitlaced old man and taken up life as a mistress. She would go that far in her degradation, she had determined, if in this act of altruism she could find a kind of peace. But when she discovered that the man who was keeping her was of all things a moneylender, she was overwhelmed with despair. The confusion in her mind was more than she herself could dispel, and she determined to reveal her feelings to her father so that he could share her distress with her.

When she arrived at the house by the pond, however, and saw with her own eyes its tranquil life, she could not bring herself to inflict this pain on the old man. Instead she determined that, bitter as it might be, she would reveal her cares to no one. With this decision Otama, who had always relied on others, for the first time learned what it meant to stand alone.

From then on, she began quietly scrutinizing her own words and actions. When Suezō came, she no longer met him with her former unreserve, but set about consciously to welcome and entertain him, putting to one side for the moment her true self. And this self laughed in ridicule at both Suezō and his plaything, Otama. When she first became aware of this change in her attitude, it disgusted her, but presently with the passage of time she grew accustomed to it and indeed began to consider it quite necessary and unavoidable.

In her attitude toward Suezō she became increasingly warm as her heart grew increasingly distant. She no longer felt grateful for his favors or indebted to him, nor could she feel pity for him that this was so. It seemed to her that, for all her lack of fine upbringing and education, she was utterly wasted on such a person. Among the people passing by her window, she began to wonder, was there not some trustworthy young man who would rescue her from her present predicament? It was when she first became aware of imaginings of this nature that she started in surprise.

Around this time, she and Okada became acquainted. At first he was no more than another student passing outside her window. She noticed that, in spite of his ruddy face and striking good looks, he displayed none of the vanity or affectation one might expect. In fact he struck her as a person of unusually attractive character. Soon she found herself wondering each day as she gazed from the window whether or not he would come by.

Though she knew neither his name nor where he lived, because of their frequent encounters she began to feel a sense of familiarity, and one day, in an unguarded moment, a lapse in her usual restraint, she smiled at him. In her shyness there was not the slightest coarse implication of proposal.

Some days later, when Okada first raised his cap in greeting, she felt her heart leap and her face grow red. Women have keen intuition. Otama knew perfectly well that when Okada doffed his cap, the action was done impulsively and with no studied intention. But she sensed that at that instant their silent, tenuous friendship, separated by the lattice of the window, had embarked upon a new phase. She could be no happier, thought Otama, as she turned over and over in her mind the picture of the young student at that moment.

★★★★★★★★

Mistresses who live under the same roof as their patron may count on the customary degree of protection. But one like Otama who lives alone faces trials the world is scarcely aware of. One day a man of about thirty, wearing a workman's coat turned inside out in the manner of an underworld character, appeared at Otama's door. He said he was from the old province of Shimōsa and was on his way home, but he had injured his foot and couldn't walk, so he would appreciate some monetary assistance.

Otama wrapped a ten-sen coin in paper and gave it to Ume to take out to the man. As he unwrapped it, he said, "What's this? Ten sen? Must be some mistake!" he added with an ugly laugh. "Better go make sure!" and he threw the money back at her.

Ume, her face red with confusion, picked it up and took it into the next room to Otama, whereupon the man brazenly followed her into the room and plopped himself down beside the brazier that Otama was just then replenishing with charcoal. He began rambling on about one thing and another, but little of what he said made sense. Repeatedly he referred to the time "when I was in the lockup"; one moment he was ordering the women around, the next moment whining about his troubles. He reeked so of wine it was enough to make one sick.

Otama was frightened almost to tears, but she managed to remain composed and, taking two of the green, card-shaped fifty-sen bills that were in circulation at that time and wrapping them in paper where he could see her, she handed them to him without a word.

The man was unexpectedly easy to satisfy. "They're little fellows, but seeing as there's two of them, they'll do nicely," he said. "You've got a lot of sense, young lady. You'll go far in the world!" Then, unsteady as he was, he trotted on his way.

Otama, greatly disturbed by this unsettling incident, decided she had better "buy" herself some neighbors in case she should need their help. She began by sending over a portion of any unusual dish she happened to prepare to the sewing teacher, who lived alone in the house on her right. Ume was dispatched to make the delivery.

The sewing teacher, a fair-complexioned woman named Otei, was over forty but retained a youthful look. She said that until she was thirty she had worked as a personal servant in the Tokyo household of the Maeda family, feudal lords in the province of Kaga. Later she married but lost her husband almost immediately. She spoke in a highly refined manner and was expert in the oieryū style of calligraphy formerly used in official documents. When Otama said she would like to learn that style of calligraphy, Otei sent over some copybooks for her to practice from.

One morning Otei appeared at Otama's kitchen door to thank her for something that Otama had sent her the day before. As the two women stood chatting a while, Otei remarked, "I see you've gotten to know Mr. Okada."

Otama did not as yet know his name, but it flashed through her mind that Otei must be referring to the student who passed by, that she had perhaps seen him greeting her, and that in such a situation, much as she hated to dissemble, she had no choice but to pretend she knew him. So, before Otei could notice her confusion, she replied, "Yes."

"Such a fine-looking young man. And a model of behavior, I'm told," said Otei.

"Do you know him well?" Otama ventured to ask.

"The lady who runs the Kamijō boardinghouse says she has lots of students in her place, but none who measure up to him!" Leaving this observation with Otama, the sewing teacher returned to her house.

Otama felt as though she herself had been praised, as she repeated over and over to herself, "Kamijō! Okada!"

Seventeen

With the passage of time Suezō's visits to Otama became not fewer but more frequent. He came not only in the evenings as he had in the past, but began dropping by at all hours during the day. He was in fact fleeing to Muenzaka from the persistent nagging of his wife, who kept demanding to know what he intended to do about her.

Suezō at such times would assure her that he was not going to do anything, that things could perfectly well go along as they were. She would insist that something had to be done, but then would complain that she no longer had her own home to return to, that she couldn't just go off and leave the children, that she was getting on in years, in effect citing all the obstacles that stood in the way of a change in her mode of living. Suezō went on reiterating that nothing need be done, but Otsune would grow more and more angry and upset till she was quite impossible to deal with. At that point Suezō would flee the house.

Accustomed to consider everything with mathematical logic, Suezō found these reproaches of Otsune's utterly incomprehensible. He felt as though he were watching the inane agonies of a person who stands facing three blank walls, a door open right behind him, and cries, "Where shall I go? I can't get out!" "The door is open! Why don't you turn around and look!" was all he had to say to such a person.

Otsune had never known an easier life; she was subject to no oppression, no restraint, no harassment whatsoever. True, there was a new factor in the situation, the woman on Muenzaka. But Suezō had not on that account grown harsh or cold toward his wife, as so many men might. On the contrary he treated Otsune with greater kindness and liberality than before. The door was standing wide open. Couldn't she see that? he wondered.

Needless to say, Suezō's way of viewing the situation was much tailored to fit his own convenience. Even though in material terms his treatment of his wife was the same as it had always been, and even though there was no change in his speech or attitude, Otama was in the picture now, and it was unreasonable to ask Otsune to pretend that things were the same as in the past. Otama was a thorn in Otsune's eye, and Suezō had no intention of plucking it out and easing Otsune's pain. Otsune had never been accustomed to analyzing matters in a logical fashion and so was perhaps not clearly conscious of all this. Yet in fact there was no door standing open behind her such as Suezō suggested. Any door that might offer Otsune peace of mind for the present and hope for the future was now hidden in deep shadow.

One morning, after quarreling with his wife, Suezō left the house in a rage sometime after ten. He thought of going straight to Muenzaka, but as luck would have it, the maid had started off with the youngest child in that direction. So to avoid a possible meeting, he skirted around Kiridōshi and, without any clear idea where he was going, walked rapidly the other way through Tenjinchō toward Gokenchō. As he hurried along, he muttered profanities under his breath.

When he crossed Shōhei Bridge, he saw a geisha coming from the opposite direction. She looked something like Otama, but observing her more closely when she passed by, he saw that her face was a mass of freckles. Oh no, he thought to himself, Otama is much better looking than that! The thought brought him an instant feeling of delight and satisfaction, and he stood for a while in the middle of the bridge peering after her. Probably out shopping, he decided, as the freckle-faced geisha disappeared down a side street of Kōbusho.

When he arrived at Megane Bridge, at that time still a new sight in the city, he turned in the direction of Yanagihara. Strolling along the riverbank, he arrived at a spot where a large umbrella had been set up under the willows. A man stood by the umbrella supervising, while a little girl of twelve or thirteen performed the then highly popular comic dance known as *kappore*. As usual, a crowd had gathered around to watch.

Suezō halted for a moment to observe the performance when a man in a workman's coat seemed about to bump right into him but then suddenly stepped aside. Suezō turned and eyed him suspiciously. For a moment their eyes met, and then the man quickly turned his back and scurried off.

"Watch out who you try that trick on!" Suezō muttered as he felt inside the breast of his kimono where he kept his wallet. Needless to say, it had not been taken. But the pickpocket should have known better than to think of such a thing. For on the days when Suezō had fought with his wife, his nerves were tense, his senses keener than ever, and he noticed many things he ordinarily might not have. Even before the pickpocket had made up his mind to try something, Suezō would have guessed what he was up to.

Suezō was proud of his powers of self-control, though at times such as this these powers were somewhat weakened. Most people would not be aware of the fact, though someone of unusually keen sensitivity might observe that Suezō was at these times a bit more glib-tongued than usual. As he went about waiting on others and addressing them with exaggerated politeness, one might detect a certain unnaturalness and perturbation in his words and actions.

It seemed as though considerable time had passed since Suezō fled from his house, and as he turned away from the riverbank, he took out his pocket watch and examined it. It was only eleven o'clock. Less than thirty minutes had passed since he left home.

Still with no destination in mind, Suezō walked through Awajichō toward Jimbōchō, striding along as though he were on important business. A little this side of Imagawa Kōji, there was at that time a shop with a sign reading "Tea and Rice." For a mere twenty sen one could get a serving of rice with pickles and tea. Suezō knew the place and thought of stopping for lunch, but decided it was too early.

Passing on, he turned right and came out in the wide street in front of Manaita Bridge. This street did not run at its full width all the way to the foot of Surugadai, as it does now. It was in fact almost a dead end, coming to a virtual stop where it turned in the direction from which Suezō had come. From there only a narrow alley ran past the shrine with calligraphy by Yamaoka Tesshu carved on its pillars. This little alley jutting off from the wide street in front of Manaita Bridge the medical students had facetiously dubbed "the vermiform appendix."

When he had crossed Manaita Bridge, Suezō noticed on the right a pet shop, noisy with the chatter of various kinds of birds. He stared for a while at the cages of parrots and macaws hanging from the eaves and at the pigeons and Korean doves below, and then turned his eyes to the cages of little birds stacked in the interior. Among the different varieties that chirped and flapped frenetically about their cages, the most conspicuous were the bright yellow canaries imported from abroad, but after watching them for a while his attention was taken by a cage of linnets. Suezō suddenly thought what a fine idea it would be to buy a pair of the little red birds and give them to Otama to take care of. They seemed just right for her.

He inquired into the price from the old proprietor, who acted less than anxious to make the sale, and bought a pair. "How will you get them home?" the proprietor asked as he took the money.

"Doesn't the cage come with them?" said Suezō in surprise, and since the man replied in the negative, he purchased a cage as well. "Can you tell if they are male and female?" Suezō inquired. The proprietor gave a faint grunt of affirmation.

Carrying the cage, Suezō left the store and turned back towards Manaita Bridge. This time he walked slowly, lifting up the cage from time to time to look at the birds. The ugly mood that had been on him since his quarrel and flight from the house appeared to have been wiped completely away, revealing a sunnier side of his disposition that was most times hidden from view.

The birds, frightened by the motion, clung to their perch, their wings folded tightly against their bodies, and made no move. Each time Suezō peered at them, he thought how nice they would look hanging in the window of the house on Muenzaka.

When he reached Imagawa Kōji, he stopped at the restaurant he had passed earlier and had lunch. He set the bird cage down on the other side of the black lacquer lunch tray that the waitress brought, his eyes admiring the pretty little birds, his mind busy with thoughts of his pretty Otama. The meal of rice and tea and pickles was simple fare at best, but Suezō ate it with relish.

Eighteen

In a quite unforeseen manner, the linnets that Suezō bought for Otama provided an opportunity for Otama and Okada to get on closer terms with one another.

I recall how the weather was that year. My father, now no longer living, was busy growing autumn flowers in the garden of our Kitasenju house. One Saturday when I came home from my lodgings at the Kamijō, I found he had bought a lot of little bamboo poles and was using them to stake up his maidenflowers and boneset plants, as *nihyaku-tōka*, the 210th day after the start of spring, was approaching, the time when typhoons were most likely to strike. That day passed without incident, but then he began worrying about the 220th day. That too came and went, but each day the clouds loomed dark and threatening. At times the weather would turn hot and muggy, as though summer had come back again, but then a strong wind would blow up from the southeast, only to die down again later. My father said we were getting the 210th-day storm in installments instead of all at once.

One Sunday evening I returned from Kitasenju to my room in the Kamijō. The other students were all away and the house was completely still. Entering my room, I sat for a while, my mind a blank, when in the next room, which I had assumed was empty, I heard a match being struck. Feeling somewhat lonely, I immediately called out, "Is that you, Okada?"

I heard something like a grunt, though I could not be sure if it was meant as a reply. Okada and I had become quite chummy and no longer bothered with the usual formalities, but this was not his customary way of answering.

If I was in a vacant mood, it appeared that Okada was too. Perhaps he's got something on his mind, I thought, and I had a sudden urge to see what his expression would be like. I called out once more. "Mind if I bother you a while?"

"Why would I mind? I just got back myself and was sitting here thinking about nothing when I heard you rattling around. Then I decided to get up and light the lamp." This time he spoke distinctly.

I stepped into the hall and opened the door to his room. The window that faced the Iron Gate was open and Okada was sitting, his elbows propped on his desk, gazing out the window. Beyond the vertical bars of the window, a few dusty cypresses growing in the area between the outer wall and the street were visible in the dusk.

Okada turned and looked at me. "It's terribly hot and sticky again today, isn't it? Some mosquitoes have gotten into my room and they're driving me crazy!"

I sat down beside Okada's desk. "You're right about the weather. My father says we're getting the 210th in installments."

"That's a novel way to put it. Maybe he's right. I was going to go out, but the sky kept clouding up and then turning clear again, and before I could decide what to do, I found I'd spent the whole morning lying around reading that copy of *Chin P'ing Mei* you lent me. Then I felt so groggy in the head I went out after lunch and met with this strange adventure." Okada did not look around but kept staring out the window as he spoke.

"What adventure is that?"

"I slew the dragon—or rather, the snake." Okada turned to face me.

"And rescued the beautiful lady?"

"No, I rescued the birds. But it had something to do with a beautiful lady."

"Sounds interesting. Tell me about it."

Nineteen

This was Okada's story.

That Sunday afternoon the clouds raced across the sky and the wind came in violent sporadic gusts, whirling up the dust in the streets. Dizzy-headed from the Chinese novel he had been reading all morning, Okada left his lodging and, having no special objective, followed his customary route, turning in the direction of Muenzaka.

His mind was still occupied with *Chin P'ing Mei*, the book he had been reading. Chinese novels, this among them, as a rule run on for ten or twelve pages in a quite ordinary manner and then, as though fulfilling a promise made to the reader, come up with a decidedly racy passage. "I'd just been reading that sort of book, you see, and I must have had a pretty stupid expression on my face as I walked along," Okada explained.

When he reached the stone wall of the Iwasaki mansion on the right, where the road sloped down sharply, he became aware of people standing in the street to his left. They were gathered in front of the house that he always looked at when he passed (though at the time Okada did not tell me why he always looked at it).

A crowd of about ten women, most of them young girls, were chattering and bustling around excitedly. Okada, unable to discern at once the cause of the commotion, left the middle of the road and walked in their direction.

The girls had their attention fixed on one object, a bird cage that hung in the lattice window of the house, and as he approached he realized there was good reason for their excitement. A little bird fluttered around the narrow cage, crying wildly. Looking more closely to determine what was frightening it, Okada saw that a large snake had thrust its head into the cage. It had managed to work its way in between the strips of thin bamboo without breaking them, so that the cage did not appear to be damaged.

Peering over the shoulders of the group, Okada stepped forward a little to get a better view when, as though by arrangement, the girls made way so he could move closer, regarding him, it seemed, as a possible rescuer. From this point he discovered something new. Besides the bird that flapped around the cage, there was another gripped in the mouth of the snake. It had died, evidently of fright; one wing was clamped in the snake's jaws, the other hung limply down.

A woman slightly older than the others, who appeared to be the lady of the house, flustered and hesitant, turned to Okada to ask if he could help.

"Everyone has been kind enough to stop work and come over from next door, but we are all women and I'm afraid there is nothing we can do," she added.

"This lady heard the birds making a noise and she opened the paper panels to look," explained one of the girls. "When she saw the snake she let out a scream. We dropped what we were doing and came running, but there's absolutely nothing we can do! Our teacher is out at the moment, but even if she were here she's probably too old to be any help." The sewing teacher closed her school every fifth day instead of on Sundays, which was why the girls were at her house that day.

At this point in his story, Okada paused to remark, "The lady of the house was quite a beauty." But he failed to mention that he had noticed her before and that he greeted her whenever he passed the house.

Before replying to the plea for help, Okada moved closer to the cage to examine the snake. It had apparently crawled along the eaves between this house and the next to reach the cage, which hung in the window opposite the sewing teacher's house. Its body was draped like a rope over the brace under the eaves, its tail still hidden behind the top of the corner pillar. It was remarkably long. Most likely it lived in the shrubbery somewhere on the Kaga estate and, sensitive to the changes in air pressure in the recent spell of unusual weather, had ventured out of its lair and happened on the bird cage. Okada considered for a moment what to do. It was no wonder that the women were helpless.

"Do you have some sort of knife?" he asked.

"Run in the kitchen and bring that carving knife," the woman said to one of the girls who seemed to be the maid. Like the girls from the sewing school, she wore a summer kimono, but her sleeves were tucked up with a purple merino cord.

The girl looked hesitantly at her mistress, reluctant, it appeared, to have the knife she customarily used to cut up fish employed for such a purpose. "It's all right," the woman added. "I'll buy you another one to use."

Okada waited impatiently till the maid brought the knife and then, slipping off his clogs, put one foot on the ledge of the bay window and gripped the eaves with his left hand. He was expert at such gymnastics. He could see that the knife, though new, was not very sharp, and so had no hopes of cutting the snake in two with a single stroke. Instead, pinning the body of the snake against the brace of the eaves, he rolled the knife back and forth several times. When the knife cut through the snake's scales, it felt as though he were shattering a piece of glass.

The snake had already half swallowed the head of the little bird and, wounded though it was, thrashed this way and that but made no move to release its prize or withdraw its head from the cage. Okada continued to saw back and forth until finally, as though slicing a piece of meat on a cutting board, he managed to cut the body in two. The hind part, still writhing, fell with a thud on the moss and stones that received the drip from the eaves. The upper half, no longer supported by the lintel of the bay window, dangled by the head from the cage. The snake's head, swollen by the half-swallowed bird in its jaws, was held fast by the bamboo bars of the cage, and the weight of the body caused the cage to tip at a forty-five degree angle. The other bird, its strength still amazingly unexhausted, continued to flutter back and forth frantically.

Okada let go the brace of the eaves and jumped down. The women had watched breathlessly up to this point, but now several of the younger ones returned to the sewing teacher's house. "You better take down the cage so I can get the snake's head out," Okada said, turning to the mistress of the house. But neither she nor the maid, staring at the drops of dark blood that dripped down from the dangling body onto the windowsill, seemed to have nerve enough to enter the house and unhook the cage from its fastening.

"Shall I take it down for you?" an excited voice called from the crowd. Everyone turned in the direction of the speaker. It was the apprentice from the saké store. While Okada had been busy with the snake, no one had passed up or down Muenzaka on this quiet Sunday afternoon but the apprentice who, happening by, his order book and rope-slung saké bottle in hand, had stopped to observe the proceedings. When the hind part of the snake fell to the ground, he set down his bottle and order book, picked up a small stone, and began poking the severed end of the snake. He watched intently while at each poke the body, life still in it, made wriggling motions.

"Oh, would you do that for us?" exclaimed the woman of the house. The maid led the boy into the house and presently he appeared at the window. Climbing onto the sill beside the potted lily, he reached up as high as he could and unhooked the cord from the nail from which it hung. Since the maid refused to touch the cage, he climbed down and carried it out by the entrance himself.

Addressing the maid in an officious tone, he said, "I'll take care of the cage. You better go wipe up the blood. Some of it got on the tatami matting too." "Oh yes, get the blood up as quickly as possible!" added the woman of the house, whereupon the maid disappeared into the house once more.

Okada examined the cage the apprentice was holding. The bird that was still alive clung to the perch, trembling all over. The body of the other bird was half hidden by the snake's jaws. Even after it had been cut in two, the snake had gone on until the very last trying to swallow the bird.

"Shall I take the snake out?" asked the boy, turning to Okada.

"That would be fine," he replied with a laugh. "But you better lift the head up to the middle of the bars and be careful not to break the bamboo when you pull it out." The boy extracted the head without difficulty and tugged at the bird in its jaws. "Even when he's dead he won't let go!" he said.

The remainder of the girls from the sewing school, convinced there was nothing further to watch, wandered back to the house next door. Okada glanced around. "I guess I'll be going too," he said.

The woman had been standing lost in thought, but when she heard this she looked at Okada. She seemed about to say something, but hesitated and turned her eyes aside. As she did so, she spied a little bit of blood on his hand. "Oh, you've got something on your hand!" she exclaimed and sent the maid inside to fetch a basin of water. The girl brought the water to the entranceway.

At this point in his story, Okada did not describe the woman's attitude in any detail, but merely remarked, "It was just a tiny speck of blood on my little finger. I'm amazed she even noticed it."

As Okada was washing his hands, the apprentice, who was still trying to pull the body of the dead bird out of the snake's jaws, suddenly shouted, "Oops!"

The woman, a clean, neatly folded towel in her hand, stood by Okada's side. One hand on the open door of the entrance, she peered out and said, "What is it now?"

The apprentice held his palm pressed against the side of the cage. "The other bird almost got out the hole where the snake's head was!" he explained.

Okada, finished washing his hands, wiped them on the towel. "Don't take your hand away!" he warned the boy, and then asked the woman for a piece of string or something he could use to mend the hole in the cage.

The woman thought a moment. "How would some paper twine do?" she asked.

"Fine," said Okada.

She told the maid to bring some of the paper twine she used to tie up her hair from the drawer of the mirror stand. The maid brought the twine and Okada laced it over the hole in the cage so that the bird could not escape.

"Well, I guess that about finishes my work," he said, stepping out the door.

"Thank you so much," said the woman, as though at a loss for further words, and she followed him out.

Okada called to the boy. "Since you're being so helpful, would you mind throwing the snake away somewhere?"

"Right! I'll throw it in a deep place in the ditch at the foot of the slope. If only I had a piece of rope to carry it with—"

"If you'll wait just a minute, we have some rope in the house," said the woman and turned to speak to the maid. During the interval Okada took his leave and, without looking back, went on down the hill.

His story concluded, Okada glanced at me and said, "Admittedly it was for a beautiful lady, but I think I did quite a lot, don't you?"

"Yes indeed. Killing a snake for the sake of a woman—it has an intriguing fairy tale air to it. But I don't think that will be the end of the story." I was just telling him frankly how I felt.

"Nonsense! If the story were unfinished, I wouldn't have told it to anyone." He did not seem to be saying this just for effect. But if this was indeed the end of the story, he must have felt a certain degree of regret.

Listening to Okada's account, I accepted it as a fairy tale of sorts. But I did not tell him what it immediately made me think of. Okada had been reading *Chin P'ing Mei*, and I wondered if he had not perhaps met up with its fatal heroine, Golden Lotus.

Every student in the university at that time was familiar with the name of Suezō, the former porter who had risen to the position of moneylender. Even those who never borrowed money had at least heard of him. But there were many who were not aware that the woman on Muenzaka was Suezō's mistress. Okada was one of these. At that time I knew little about Otama's background, but I did know that it was Suezō who had established her in the house next to the sewing teacher's. As far as possession of the facts went, I was a step ahead of Okada.

Twenty

It was the day Okada killed the snake for her. Otama, who until then had exchanged only glances and nods with the student, felt, after their intimate encounter over the snake, a dramatic change in her emotions, one that surprised even her.

For all women, there are things they regard as desirable but which they do not feel compelled to purchase. Such objects—a watch, a ring, displayed in the window of a store—they will invariably stop to look at as they pass. They do not go purposely to the store to see them, but, happening along on some other errand, they will nevertheless pause for a moment of inspection. Their desire to possess the object, and their resignation to the fact that they can never afford to do so, combine to produce not distress but rather a subtle, sweet sensation of grief that women look on as a kind of joy.

The situation is quite different, however, when a woman makes up her mind to possess a thing. The emotion then is one of intense anguish. She thinks of the object until she can think of nothing else. Even if she learned that in a few days it would come easily into her hands, she could not bear to wait. Heedless of heat or cold, darkness or storm, she will lay her impulsive plans for the acquisition. Those women who in such cases resort to shoplifting are not necessarily cut from a different cloth; they are merely a little hazy as to where one draws the line between ability to purchase and desire for possession. For Otama, the student Okada had until now been no more than an object of vague desire, but suddenly she realized that she wanted him for her own.

Somehow, she felt, through the incident of the little birds, she could come closer to him. At first she thought she would buy him a gift to express her thanks and have Ume take it to him at his lodging. But what should she buy? Perhaps some country-style bean-jam cakes from Fujimura. No, that was too common and betrayed a lack of thought. She might get some material and sew him a little cushion to rest his arm on, but that would look rather like the token of sentiment one might receive from a schoolgirl sweetheart. She could not seem to hit on a good idea. And even if she settled on an appropriate item, should she just have Ume take it to him?

She had recently had some new name cards printed up in Nakachō, and she would send one along with the gift. But just a name card would not do. She would like to write a short note as well, but she had not gone beyond grade school and had had no time thereafter to work on her calligraphy, so that she did not feel she could write a satisfactory letter. Perhaps she could get the sewing teacher, who used to be employed by a family of the aristocracy, to write it for her. No. Although she of course intended to say nothing that could not be shown to others, she did not care to have anyone know that she had sent a letter to Mr. Okada. What should she do? She turned the question over and over in her mind as she put on her makeup and gave instructions in the kitchen, forgetting it for a moment and then recalling it again.

While she was at this, Suezō arrived. As she poured a cup of saké for him, she remembered her problem again. "What are you thinking so hard about?" Suezō asked.

"Why, I'm not thinking of anything," she replied with a vacant smile, but her heart began to pound. Suezō had of late become unusually acute in his observations, and it was not easy to conceal from him the fact that she had something on her mind.

After he had gone, Otama fell asleep and dreamt she bought a box of cakes and hurriedly sent Ume with it to Okada's lodging.

She woke suddenly from the dream when she realized that she had enclosed with the box neither a name card nor a note.

The next day either Okada did not go for a walk or she somehow missed his passing, for she went through the day without a glimpse of the face she longed to see. The day after, he passed the window as usual, but the house was quite dark and, though he glanced toward the window, he apparently did not see her there. The following day, as the time drew near when he customarily passed, Otama took a straw broom and began sweeping the already spotless entryway and moving a pair of wooden clogs from the left side to the right and then back again to the left.

"I'll do that!" cried Ume, emerging from the kitchen.

"Don't you bother," Otama replied. "You watch the things on the stove. I'm just doing this because I have nothing else to do." At that moment Okada came by and raised his cap in greeting. Otama stood stiffly with the broom in her hand, her face reddening and, unable to say a word, allowed him to pass by. Then she threw down the broom as though it were a burning brand, slipped out of her sandals and disappeared into the house.

What an utter fool I am! she thought as she sat by the brazier fiddling with the tongs. It was so cool today I thought it would look strange if I had the window open, so I went to all the trouble of pretending to sweep, and then when the time came I couldn't say a thing! No matter how awkward I feel in front of Suezō, I always manage to speak up if I put my mind to it.

Why couldn't I say something to Mr. Okada? After he was so kind the other day, it was only right that I should thank him. That may be the last chance I ever have to speak to him. I wanted to send Ume with a present of some sort but I haven't managed to do that, and then when I see him face to face I can't even speak out—what's wrong with me!

Why couldn't I speak to him then? I surely intended to say something, but I didn't know just how to begin. I could hardly say "Excuse me," as though I were trying to get his attention when we were already looking right at one another. It's no wonder I hesitated. Thinking it over now, I still don't know what I should have said. But to behave like such a fool! There was really no need to say anything. I should have just run out in the street. Then he would have stopped, and when he did that, I could have begun, "You were such a help the other day when that dreadful thing happened—"

As Otama sat toying with the fire in the brazier and mulling these thoughts over, the lid of the iron kettle on the trivet began bobbing up and down. She moved the lid to one side so the steam could escape.

Otama decided that she must settle on one of two alternatives, either speak to Okada herself or send Ume with a message. The evenings were growing so cool it was hardly possible to leave the paper panels of the window open. Up to now, the garden had been swept only once in the morning, but after the recent incident with the broom, Ume had taken to sweeping it again in the evening, so Otama could no longer use that as an excuse to be outside. She had tried going to the public bath at a later hour, hoping she would run into Okada along the way. But the distance to the bath at the foot of the slope was too short and she never succeeded in doing so. And as for sending Ume with a message, the longer she put that off, the more contrived it would seem.

Then she tried for a time looking at it this way, hoping to persuade herself it was all right to take no action at all. I have let all this time go by without thanking Mr. Okada, she reminded herself. In failing to express thanks where thanks were surely due, I have shown that I am willing to be indebted to him. And he must surely realize that I do in fact feel indebted to him. So, rather than expressing my thanks in a clumsy manner, it is perhaps better to leave things as they are.

Yet Otama longed to use this very indebtedness as a means to get to know Okada better as soon as possible. Only she could not hit on the exact procedure to follow, and this was a source of secret anxiety to her each day.

Otama was a woman of strong spirit. Though little time had passed since she became Suezō's mistress, she had experienced the bitterness that goes with that position, outwardly despised by those around her, secretly envied, and in turn had learned to cultivate a kind of contempt for the world that would treat her so. But she was good at heart and had not yet had time to become utterly hardened by life, and the idea of trying to become intimate with Okada, a student living in a boardinghouse, seemed to present fearful difficulties.

There was a spell of warm autumn weather that permitted her to open the window, so that each day she could at least exchange nods with Okada. But although at the time of the snake incident she had been able to speak with him in an intimate manner, and had even had occasion to hand him a towel, this did not seem to have advanced their acquaintance by any appreciable degree. Instead they reverted to their earlier formality, as though nothing had passed between them, leaving Otama feeling highly vexed.

When Suezō came to see her and they sat chatting on opposite sides of the brazier, she would think to herself, If only this were Mr. Okada! The first time she caught herself doing this, she was shocked by her own duplicity. But gradually she became quite accustomed to thinking about Okada while she carried on her conversation with Suezō. Even when Suezō made love to her, she would shut her eyes and imagine it was Okada. Sometimes she would dream that she and Okada were together. They had come together, it seemed, without any sort of bothersome procedure. How wonderful! she would think, and then all at once her companion was no longer Okada but Suezō. She would wake with a start, her nerves so taut it was impossible to get back to sleep, and weep with irritation.

And then, before one knew it, it was November. The warm autumn weather came once more and Otama could leave the window open without attracting notice, and thus could see Okada's face each day. Earlier, when two or three days of chilly rain had made this impossible and prevented her from seeing him, she had been downcast. Gentle-natured as she was, however, she never took out her frustration on Ume or made unreasonable demands. And of course she never showed a sulky face when she was around Suezō. If she felt out of sorts, she would merely plant her elbows on the rim of the brazier and gaze around in silence, till Ume would ask if perhaps she was coming down with something.

But now she saw Okada every day, and as a result was in wonderfully buoyant spirits. One morning, leaving the house in an unusually jaunty mood, she set off to visit her father at his place by the pond.

Otama visited her father once a week without fail, but on no occasion had she ever stayed more than an hour. Her father would not permit it. He was invariably kind and thoughtful, and if he happened to have something good to eat on hand, would serve it with the tea. But once that was done he would urge her to be on her way. This was not just an expression of the old man's impatience; he felt that, since he had placed his daughter in another man's service, it would be inexcusable if he detained her at his place for selfish reasons.

The second or third time Otama came to visit, she assured her father that Suezō never called on her in the morning and therefore she need not hurry off. But her father would hear none of this. "Perhaps he's never come to your place at that hour. But you have no way of knowing when he may have affairs that oblige him to do so. If you had told him in advance and gotten permission, that would be different. But when you drop in like this on your way home from shopping, you have no business staying a long while. If he begins wondering where you are spending your time you'll have only yourself to blame!"

Otama constantly worried that her father might be very much disturbed if he learned what Suezō's real occupation was, and each time she visited him she looked for signs of a change in his attitude. But her father appeared to be totally ignorant of the truth. This was not surprising. Shortly after moving to the house by the pond, he began borrowing books from a book-lending store. During the day he was always to be found with his glasses on, reading one of these.

The only kind of books he borrowed were hand-written copies of historical narratives, the sort that purport to be wholly factual. At the moment he was reading *Mikawa gofūdoki*, which describes the rise of the Tokugawa family to power. It was a work in numerous volumes and would obviously keep him happily occupied for some time. Whenever the book lender attempted to interest him in a work of fiction, he would reject the offer with scorn, saying he had no use for "made-up stories."

By evening his eyes would be tired, and instead of reading he would go to the variety theater, where he listened to comic stories or ballad-dramas. In the case of the theater, it did not seem to matter whether the stories were true or made-up. But he seldom went to the theater in Hirokōji, which most of the time featured historical recitations, unless the reciter was a particular favorite of his. These were his sole diversions. He did not believe in engaging others in what he called "useless conversation," and hence made few friends. References to Suezō's means of livelihood were thus hardly likely to reach his ears.

But there were persons in the neighborhood who wondered who the attractive young woman was that visited the old man, and they in time succeeded in finding out that she was the mistress of a moneylender. If the parties living on either side of Otama's father had been of a gossipy nature, they would no doubt have forced their unwelcome rumors on him no matter how disinclined he was to listen. Fortunately, however, the neighbor on one side was a minor museum employee who spent his time practicing calligraphy with the aid of copybooks, while on the other side was a woodblock engraver, continuing to practice his craft rather than abandon it for the more profitable seal engraving. Neither was the type likely to disturb the old man's peace of mind. At this time the only houses along the street that had been converted to commercial use were the Rengyokuan, specializing in buckwheat noodle dishes, a store selling rice cakes, and farther along toward the corner of Hirokōji, a comb store called Jūsanya.

When the old man heard someone come in the lattice door, if he caught the sound of light wooden clogs, he knew even before he heard her soft voice that Otama had come. Setting aside the copy of *Mikawa gofūdoki* he was reading and removing his glasses, he waited in happy anticipation, for a day when he could see his beloved daughter's face was for him a festive occasion. He always took off his glasses when she came. He could have seen her better with them on, but they imposed a sort of barrier that displeased him. Invariably he had a store of things he wanted to talk to her about, and after she had gone he would remember some item or other he had forgotten to mention. But he never forgot to inquire about Suezō. "And how is that fine gentleman getting along?" he would ask.

Otama, observing that her father was in an excellent mood today, let him tell her about Acha, the famous lady-in-waiting to the Tokugawa family, who was described at length in the book he was reading, and to regale her with some huge rice crackers he had bought at a branch of the Ōsenju bakery that had opened in Hirokōji. And when from time to time he asked, "Hadn't you better be going now?" she replied with a laugh, "It's still early!" and stayed on till almost noon. Had she mentioned that Suezō was likely to drop by at unexpected hours these days, she knew his inquiries would take on an even more anxious tone. As for herself, she had grown so indifferent that it did not bother her to think Suezō might call when she was out.

Twenty-One

The weather turned colder and in the mornings the planks that covered the drain from Otama's house were white with frost. The long rope that hauled up water from the well was icy, and Otama, feeling sorry for Ume, bought her a pair of work gloves to wear. But Ume, thinking she could never carry out her kitchen chores if she was forever putting them on and taking them off, instead stored them away carefully and went on drawing water with her bare hands. When there was laundry to do or mopping with a wet rag, Otama heated water for Ume to use, but bit by bit Ume's hands grew red and chapped.

This troubled Otama. "Whenever you've had your hands in water, you mustn't leave them wet," she said. "Be sure to dry them right away. And when you've finished what you're doing, don't forget to wash them with soap," she added, giving the maid a cake of soap she had bought. But still, to Otama's distress, Ume's hands continued to get redder and rougher. In the past Otama had done the same sort of work herself, and she wondered why her hands had never gotten chapped like Ume's.

Otama had always been in the habit of getting up as soon as she woke in the morning. But these days, when Ume would call to her, "There's ice on the wash basin! Why don't you stay in bed a little longer," Otama would pull the quilt more tightly around her. When you get in bed go straight to sleep! the pedagogues admonish young people, and get up as soon as you wake! For they know that from youthful bodies lolling in the warmth of covers can spring the flowers of evil fantasy. Lying in bed at such times, Otama would indeed surrender herself to unbridled imaginings; her eyes would take on a special gleam, and a redness as though from wine would spread from her eyelids down over her cheeks.

One frosty morning following a night of clear skies and brightly gleaming stars, Otama was lying in bed in her newly learned indolence. Ume had long since opened the shutters, and now the morning sun streamed in the front window. Observing this, Otama finally got up and, tying her kimono with a narrow sash and slipping on a short coat, went to the verandah to brush her teeth. As she did so, she heard the lattice door open and Ume's voice calling politely, "Good morning, sir," followed by the footsteps of someone entering.

"Sleepyhead!" exclaimed Suezō as he sat down by the brazier.

"Excuse me a moment, will you? I had no idea you would be coming so early!" said Otama, hastily putting down her toothbrush and emptying her mouth into the wash basin. Her confused, smiling face seemed to Suezō more beautiful than ever. Indeed she had grown lovelier each day since she had moved to Muenzaka. The girlish charm that had first attracted him had these days given way to an air of enchanting maturity. The change, mused Suezō with pride, sprang from her new understanding of love, the understanding that he himself had taught her.

But Suezō's penetrating eyes had in this case woefully misread the facts. Otama had at first served her patron faithfully and wholeheartedly. But with the rapid changes in her way of life, the anxieties and periods of deep reflection, she had learned at last a kind of artfulness; there was in her heart now something like the hard-won dispassionate coldness of a woman who has known many men. And as she became more cunning in her heart, she grew more careless in her ways, and this very carelessness acted on Suezō as a delightful stimulus, spurring his passion to greater intensity. Though he did not correctly divine the causes for the change, he responded warmly to the new attraction that it brought.

Otama crouched down and drew the wash basin to her side. "Would you turn the other way for a moment?" she said.

"Why?" asked Suezō, lighting a cigarette.

"I have to wash my face."

"Well, go on and wash it."

"But I can't if you're watching!"

"How difficult you are! Is this all right?" he asked, turning his back to the verandah and continuing to smoke, amazed at her childishness.

Otama did not wash her body, but only lowered the collar of her kimono a short way and scrubbed her face busily. She did not wash as thoroughly as usual, but since she had no blemishes that needed to be disguised with makeup, there was no reason why she should mind if anyone watched.

Suezō sat looking the other way for a while, but soon resumed his former position. Otama, busy with her washing, was not aware of the change until she pulled the mirror stand toward her and spied his face, the cigarette in his mouth.

"Aren't you terrible!" she said, but without further comment began arranging her hair. The collar of her robe, tipped back from her neck, showed a triangle of pale skin, and as she raised her arms he could see a few inches of plump upper arm, sights that never failed to delight him.

Thinking that if he waited in silence she might feel obliged to hurry, Suezō said in a genial voice, "You don't have to rush. I didn't come for any particular reason. I told you the other day I would come tonight. But as it happens, I have to go out to Chiba. If everything goes well, I'll be back tomorrow. It's just possible, though, that it may be the day after."

"Oh?" Otama exclaimed, wiping her comb and turning to look at him. Her face wore an uneasy expression.

"Wait for me like a good girl," he said with a laugh and, putting away his cigarette case, got up to leave.

"But you haven't even had a cup of tea!" she protested, throwing down the comb and jumping up to see him off. By that time Suezō was already opening the lattice door.

Ume brought the breakfast tray from the kitchen and set it down. "I'm terribly sorry," she said, bowing apologetically.

Otama, sitting by the brazier and using the fire tongs to rake off the ashes that covered the live coals, looked up with a smile. "What are you sorry about?"

"I mean I was too late in making the tea," the girl replied.

"Oh that!" said Otama as she picked up her chopsticks. "I only said that to have something to say. I'm sure he didn't think anything about it."

Ume, observing her mistress as she ate breakfast, noted that, although of a generally sunny disposition, she seemed even more cheerful than usual. About Otama's faintly red cheeks the shadow of the smile she had given in answer to the maid's apology still lingered. Ume considered for a moment the possible reasons for such good spirits, but unable in her naiveté to reach any conclusion, she was content merely to reflect in her own mood a similar feeling of cheer.

Otama looked sharply at Ume and, in a voice more pleasant than ever, said, "Wouldn't you like to go see your family?"

Ume stared in astonishment. The year was 1880 and in the households of Tokyo the customs of earlier feudal times remained largely in effect; even servants whose families lived in the city were rarely allowed to return home to visit at any time other than the regular semiannual holidays. "I don't think the master will come this evening, so you may go home and spend the night if you like," Otama continued.

"May I really?" exclaimed Ume, not out of doubt but from a sense of overwhelming gratitude.

"Now would I lie to you or do anything bad like teasing?" said Otama. "You needn't bother with the breakfast things. Just run along and have a good time. You can spend the night, but be sure to be back early in the morning."

"Oh yes!" said Ume, her face reddening with delight. And through her mind flashed a rapid succession of images, like scenes in a shadow play: her father, a rickshaw puller, two or three rickshaws lined up in the dirt-floored entrance; her father, in between runs, resting on a cushion in the cramped area between the chest of drawers and the brazier; her mother, seated in the same narrow area when her father was out, a lock of hair dangling down over one cheek, her sleeves seldom loosened from the sash that held them tucked up while she worked.

Although Otama had said she need not bother to clean up, Ume decided at least to wash the dishes and, pouring hot water into a shallow wooden tub, she rattled the bowls and plates through it.

Otama appeared in the kitchen with something wrapped in paper. "Here you are doing things!" she exclaimed. "There are hardly any dishes—I can do them. You fixed your hair last night so it's all right as it is. Run now and change your kimono. Oh, and here's something to take to your family in place of a proper present." She handed the paper packet to the girl. Inside was one of the card-shaped, green half-yen notes.

After she had hurried Ume on her way, Otama briskly tucked up her sleeves and the ends of her skirt and went into the kitchen where, as though engaged in the most fascinating task, she began to wash again the bowls and plates that Ume had already done. A veteran at such work, she could have finished them with twice the speed and efficiency of the maid. But today, like a child with a set of toys, she dabbled leisurely over them. Holding a single plate in her hand for five minutes, she stared up at the sky, her face livened with a pale red glow. And through her mind passed a succession of the most delightful images.

A woman, in any matter whatsoever, will hesitate with pitiful irresolution until she has made up her mind. Once having done so, however, she looks neither to right or left, as a man might, but, like a horse with blinders on, plods steadily toward her goal. Across the path of a thoughtful man lie obstacles of doubt and trepidation that to a woman are no more than dust in the road. Daring things he will not dare, she often succeeds quite beyond expectation.

A third party viewing Otama's efforts to approach Okada might have wearied of their vacillating slowness. But this morning, with Suezō's departure for Chiba, Otama sped like a ship before a fair wind toward the shore of her destination. She had hurried Ume off to her parents' place, where the girl would spend the night. And Suezō, who might otherwise obstruct her plans, would be staying the night in Chiba. Now, with all possible restraints and hindrances removed for the day, she felt an uncontrollable joy. For she sensed in this unexpected freedom an omen of certain and easy success.

Today Mr. Okada would surely pass by. Often he passed the house twice, so even if she should somehow miss him on his way down the hill, she would certainly meet him as he came back. And today, at whatever cost, she would speak to him without fail. She would speak without fail, and he would of course stop to listen.

She had sunk to the position of a mistress, she told herself, the mistress of a moneylender. But she was not ugly. In fact she was better looking now than when she was just a girl. And she had come to realize, albeit through bitter experience, that she was appealing to men. Mr. Okada could not think her completely hateful. Of that she was certain. If he did, he would not nod each time he saw her face, nor indeed would he have killed the snake for her. If that had happened at someone else's house, he would probably have gone right by without bothering to stop. And although she had not made her feelings entirely clear to him, he could not be wholly unaware of them. Things often turn out to be much easier than one anticipates.

As Otama's thoughts raced along in this fashion, the water in the wooden tub grew cold, but she was unconscious of the change.

She put the breakfast tray on the shelf and sat down beside the brazier, fidgeting restlessly. For a while she considered smoothing again the ashes that Ume had already neatly raked. Then abruptly she stood up and began to change her clothes. She was going to the hair-dresser in Dōbōchō. The woman who came regularly to the house to do her hair had kindly recommended a woman in Dōbōchō "for special occasions," but until now Otama had had no reason to go to her.

Twenty-Two

There is a story in a Western-language children's book called something like "Because of One Nail." I do not recall it exactly, but it is about how, because one nail in a cartwheel is missing, a farmer's son riding in a cart meets up with all sorts of difficulties. In my present story, it was a dish of mackerel boiled in *miso* sauce that played the part of the "one nail."

In the days when I was surviving on the food served in boardinghouses and student dormitories, I encountered one dish that completely turned my stomach. To this day, no matter how pleasant and airy the dining room or how clean the table setting, if I once catch sight of this dish, I seem to smell once more that indescribably nauseating odor that I knew long ago in the dormitory dining room. Even other kinds of fish cooked with seaweed or gluten bread will remind me of that awful smell and I react as strongly as if the dish were actually mackerel in *miso* sauce.

And mackerel in *miso* sauce was what we were served that evening in the Kamijō boardinghouse. Usually as soon as the maid brought the dinner tray to my room, I was grabbing for the chopsticks. This

146.

evening, noting my hesitation, she said, "Don't you like mackerel?"

"I have no objection to mackerel. If it's boiled I can eat it fine, but not boiled in *miso* sauce!"

"The landlady must not have known that. Maybe I can get you some eggs," she said, about to leave.

"Wait," I said. "I'm not really hungry now. I think I'll go for a walk. Don't say anything to the landlady. I don't want her to think I don't like the cooking and cause her a lot of worry."

"Still, it's too bad—"

"Nonsense," I said, getting up to put on my *hakama*. Seeing me do so, the maid picked up the tray and left.

"Okada, are you in?" I called to the room next door.

"Yes. Do you want something?" came the reply.

"Nothing special. I just thought I'd take a walk and on the way back perhaps stop at the Toyokuniya for something to eat. Want to come along?"

"Let's go," he replied. "I have something I want to talk to you about anyway."

I took my cap from the nail where it hung and together we left the boardinghouse. I think it was a little after four. We had not discussed which direction to take, but once out the door we both turned to the right.

As we started down the Muenzaka slope, I nudged Okada with my elbow. "There she is!" I said.

"What?" said Okada, though he knew perfectly well what I meant, and turned to look at the house on the left with the lattice door.

Otama stood in front of the house. Even in ill health she would have been beautiful, but in fact she was young and healthy, and today her usual good looks had been heightened by careful makeup and grooming. To my eyes she seemed to possess a beauty wholly beyond anything I had noted earlier, and her face shone with a kind of radiance. The effect was dazzling.

As though in a trance, Otama fixed her eyes on Okada. He raised his cap in a flustered greeting and then unconsciously quickened his pace.

With the unreserve of a third party, I turned several times to look back. She watched us for a long time.

Okada, his eyes glued to the ground, continued his hurried pace to the bottom of the hill. I followed along in silence, troubled by a number of conflicting emotions. Dominant among them was the feeling that I would very much like to be in Okada's place. But my conscious mind was loathe to admit this fact. I'm not that kind of contemptible fellow! I told myself firmly, and did my best to suppress the thought. Failing in my efforts to do so, I began to fume.

When I say I wished I were in Okada's place, I do not mean I wanted to surrender myself to the woman's enticements. Only I thought how delightful it must be to be loved, as Okada was, by such a beautiful woman. What would I do if I were the object of such ardor? I would want to reserve the liberty to decide that when the occasion arose. But I definitely would not flee the way Okada had. I would meet with the woman and talk. I would not do anything reprehensible, of course, just meet with her and talk. And I would love her as I would a younger sister. I would put all my strength at her disposal. And somehow I would rescue her from her sordid surroundings. My imaginings raced on until they reached this fanciful conclusion.

Okada and I walked along in silence till we arrived at the intersection at the foot of the slope. Once we had passed the police box there, I finally spoke up. "This is a fine state of affairs, I must say!"

"What's that?"

"What do you mean, what's that? You've been thinking about that woman all along, haven't you! I turned around a couple of times to see, and she just kept on looking in your direction. She's probably still looking this way. It's like that man in the *Tso chuan* who 'gazed at the woman as she approached and looked after her as she passed.' Only in this case the roles are reversed."

"Let's not talk about her," Okada said. "You're the only person I've told that story to. You can leave off joking about it from now on."

As he said this, we reached the edge of the pond, where both of us paused for a moment. "Shall we go that way?" Okada asked, pointing toward the north end of the pond.

"Fine," I said and, turning left, we started circling the pond. After we had gone some ten paces, I noticed a row of two-story houses on the left. More or less to myself I remarked, "That's where Mr. Fukuchi, the writer, and the moneylender Suezō live."

"They make an odd combination, don't they," Okada remarked. "Though I hear Fukuchi's reputation isn't all that savory either."

For no particular reason I felt like arguing the point. "If you go into politics as Fukuchi has, people are bound to spread stories, no matter what." Probably I wanted to emphasize as much as possible the distance that separated the two men.

Two or three houses north of the fence surrounding the Fukuchi mansion was a little house that at the time of my story displayed a sign reading "Freshwater Fish." Spotting it, I said, "From the sign, you'd guess they must serve you fish right out of the pond here."

"That's what I was thinking. But it's probably not quite the sort of pondside tavern where the heroes of *The Water Margin* used to meet."

By this time we had crossed the little bridge on the north side of the pond. On the bank of the pond a young man stood looking intently at something. As we drew nearer, he called, "Hi there!" It was Ishihara, a fellow student who was much involved in jujitsu but who never read any books other than those assigned in his courses. Because of this difference in tastes, neither Okada nor I were particularly friendly with him, though we did not dislike him either.

"What are you looking at?" I asked.

Ishihara silently pointed toward the pond. Okada and I peered through the gray-tinged evening air in the direction he indicated. At the time of my story the whole surface of the pond from the little ditch that runs down from Nezu to the shore where the three of us were standing was overgrown with reeds. The dead leaves of the reeds gradually thinned out toward the center of the pond, where ragged dried-up lotus leaves and sponge-shaped seed pods dotted the surface, their stems, broken at varying heights, slanting down into the water at sharp angles and giving the scene a desolate air. Ten or twelve wild geese moved to and fro among the soot-colored stems of the lotuses, gliding over the black, faintly glimmering surface of the pond. A few of them sat motionless where they were.

"Do you think you could throw a stone that far?" asked Ishihara, looking at Okada.

"I could throw that far all right, but whether I could hit anything is another matter," Okada replied.

"Try it and see."

Okada hesitated. "The birds are sleeping. It would be a shame to throw stones at them."

Ishihara laughed. "Let's not get too tenderhearted now. If you don't want to throw a stone, then I will."

Okada reluctantly picked up a stone. "In that case I'll throw a stone to chase them away." The stone made a faint whizzing sound as it flew through the air. As I stared fixedly in the direction it had gone, I saw the raised head of one of the wild geese slump forward. At the same instant two or three other geese, beating their wings and crying, skittered away over the surface of the water. The goose with the crumpled head remained where it was.

"You hit it!" Ishihara exclaimed. Then, after studying the surface of the pond for a while, he added. "I can get that goose for you. But you'll have to give me a little help."

"How are you going to get it?" Okada asked. Curious to know what he would answer, I listened closely.

"Right now is a bad time. In another thirty minutes it will be dark. Once it gets dark, I can get it with no trouble. You don't have to do anything special. Just be here when the time comes and do as I tell you. A wild goose makes very tasty eating!" said Ishihara.

"Sounds interesting," remarked Okada. "But what will we do till the thirty minutes are up?"

"I'll hang around here. But you two better go somewhere else. Three people together here would be too conspicuous."

"In that case you and I better take a turn around the lake," I said to Okada.

"Fine with me," Okada agreed and started walking.

Twenty-Three

Okada and I skirted the edge of Hanazonochō, walking in the direction of the flight of stone steps that leads up to the Tōshōgū Shrine. For a while both of us remained silent. Then Okada, as if talking to himself, said, "Some wild geese are just unlucky." Though there was no logical connection, the image of the woman on Muenzaka flashed through my mind.

"All I did was throw in the direction where the geese were," said Okada, this time speaking to me.

"Sure," I said, continuing to think about the woman. "Still," I added after a moment, "I'd like to see how Ishihara goes about retrieving it."

"Sure," Okada agreed as he walked along lost in thought. Probably he was still feeling bad about the wild goose.

The two of us turned south at the foot of the stone stairs and walked toward the Benten Shrine; the death of the wild goose seemed to have cast a deep shadow over us, and our conversation kept lapsing into silence. When we passed in front of the torii gate leading to the Benten Shrine, Okada, apparently determined to turn the discussion in another direction, said, "There was something I wanted to talk to you about." What he had to tell me came as a complete surprise.

He had intended to come to my room tonight, he said, but since I'd invited him for a walk, he had come along. He thought he would talk to me over dinner, but it looked as though that would be impossible. So while we were walking along he would sum up the situation.

He had decided not to wait for graduation but to go abroad; he had already obtained a passport from the Ministry of Foreign Affairs and notified the university that he was withdrawing. A certain Professor W. from Germany who was in Japan to study endemic diseases of East Asia had hired Okada as an assistant, agreeing to pay him 4,000 marks to cover his fare to Germany and back and a monthly stipend of 200 marks. He had been looking for a student who knew German and was also competent in reading texts in Chinese, and Professor Baelz had recommended Okada.

Okada had called on Professor W. in his quarters in Tsukiji and been given an examination. He was asked to translate two or three lines from the early Chinese medical texts *Su-wen* and *Nan-chinq* and five or six lines from later works such as *Shanq-han-lun* and *Pinq-yüan hou-lun*. As luck would have it, the *Nan-ching* passage contained the term *san-chiao* or "three *chiao*" and Okada had wondered how in the world he would translate it, since there is no equivalent in Western medical terminology, but he ended up just calling it "three *chiao*." Anyway, he had passed the exam and been given a contract on the spot.

Professor W. was on the faculty of the same Leipzig university that Professor Baelz was affiliated with, so he would take Okada with him to Leipzig and help him with his doctoral exams. As a graduation thesis Okada had been told he could submit the translations of Chinese medical texts that he prepared for Professor W.

Okada announced he was leaving the Kamijō the following morning and moving to Professor W.'s quarters in Tsukiji, where he would pack up the books that Professor W. had collected in China and Japan. He would then accompany Professor W. on an inspection tour of Kyushu, and from Kyushu proceed directly to Europe via a ship of the Messagerie Maritime Line.

I interrupted every now and then to exclaim, "What a surprise!" or "You don't waste time, do you!" and it seemed as though I had been listening to his explanation for quite a while. When he finished and I looked at my watch, however, I found that only ten minutes had passed since we left Ishihara. And we had already gone two-thirds of the way around the lake and were coming to the end of Ikenohata. "If we go on like this we'll get there too early," I said.

"Why not stop at the Rengyokuan for a bowl of noodles?" Okada suggested.

I immediately agreed to that, and we turned back in the direction of the Rengyokuan. At that time it was rated the best noodle restaurant in the entire Shitaya-Hongō area.

Over his noodles, Okada went on with his story. "Since I've come this far, it's a shame not to graduate. But I would never qualify for a government grant to study abroad, so if I let this chance slip by I'll never get to Europe."

"You're right. You can't afford to pass it up. What does it matter about graduation? If you get a doctorate over there, it'll be the same thing. And even if you don't get a doctorate, you won't have any worries."

"That's how I look at it too. Just so I get the qualifications I need. I'll go that far as a 'concession to custom,' to use the Chinese phrase."

"But if you're leaving so soon, what about preparations?"

"I'll go just as I am. Professor W. says that Western-style clothes made in Japan are no good when you get to Europe anyway."

"Is that right? I read in *Kagetsu shinshi* that once when the journalist Narushima Ryūhoku was in Yokohama, he suddenly decided to go abroad and went right aboard the ship there."

"Yes, I read that too. He left without even writing to his family. At least I've told my family all about my plans."

"Is that so? I really envy you! Going with Professor W., you won't have to worry about any complications along the way. But what kind of trip will it be? I can't even imagine."

"I don't know either. But yesterday I went to see Professor Shibata Shōkei. He's helped me in the past and I wanted to tell him about my trip. He gave me a guidebook he wrote for people going abroad."

"There are books like that?"

"It's not for sale. He says he just hands it out to yokels like me."

While we were exchanging these remarks, I looked at my watch and discovered we had only five minutes left before the thirty were up. Hurrying out of the Rengyokuan, Okada and I went to where Ishihara was waiting. Darkness had by now shrouded the pond and the vermilion of the Benten Shrine was only faintly visible through the evening mist.

"The time's just right," said Ishihara, pulling us to the edge of the water. "All the other geese have gone to roost, so I'll get straight to work. You two have to stand here and give me directions. See that lotus stem bent to the right about twenty feet out? And the shorter one bent to the left in line with it farther out? I have to

158.

stay directly in line with those two points. If you see me varying from that line, tell me which way to go so I get back in line."

"Right," said Okada. "The parallax principle. But isn't the water going to be deep?"

"It certainly won't be over my head," said Ishihara as he quickly stripped off his clothes.

At the spot where he entered, the mud came only to his knees. Lifting his legs high out of the water like a heron, he moved forward with a sloshing sound. In places the water seemed to be deeper, then it got shallow again. Soon he had moved out beyond the two lotuses. A moment later Okada called, "Right!" and Ishihara bore to the right. "Left!" shouted Okada, seeing that Ishihara was bearing too far right. Suddenly Ishihara halted and bent over. Then he began retracing his steps. As he passed the farther of the two lotuses, we could see he was holding something in his right hand.

Ishihara returned to the embankment with only a little mud on his thighs. In his hand he held an unexpectedly large wild goose. After rapidly washing his legs, he put on his clothes. In those days this part of the lake had few visitors; from the time Ishihara entered the water until he returned with his prize, not a soul had passed by.

"How are we going to carry it?" I asked as Ishihara stepped into his *hakama*.

"Okada has the biggest cloak, so he can hide it under his cloak. We'll cook it at my place."

Ishihara rented a room in a private house and the landlady, an older woman, had the advantage of being less than exacting in her morals. So if we gave her a portion of our catch, she was unlikely to say anything about where it came from. The house was on a remote, winding alley that led off from Yushima Kiridōshi and came out back of the Iwasaki mansion.

Ishihara explained briefly how we could get there with our goose. There were two possible ways to approach the house, a southern route by way of Kiridōshi, and a northern route via Muenzaka, both of them circling around the Iwasaki estate. The distance was approximately the same either way, so that was no consideration. The problem was getting past the police box; there was one of those on either route.

Calculating the advantages of each, we decided to avoid the busy Kiridōshi approach and take the much less frequented one via Muenzaka. The best plan seemed to have Okada carry the goose under his cloak, with the two of us flanking him and shielding him from scrutiny.

With a strained smile Okada thrust the bird under his cloak, but however he held it, the feathers stuck out two or three inches below the bottom of the cloak. In addition, the lower part of the cloak was puffed out in a peculiar fashion, so that Okada was shaped like a cone. Ishihara and I would have to make sure his odd contours did not attract attention.

Twenty-Four

"Here we go now!" said Ishihara as he and I took our places on either side of Okada and started walking. All three of us were worrying about how we would get past the police box at the foot of Muenzaka. To prepare us for the ordeal, Ishihara launched into a voluble lecture. As far as I could make out, it had to do with stability of mind. Failure to maintain proper stability of mind created an opening, and where there was an opening, one could be taken advantage of. He used as an example the story of how a tiger will not eat a drunken man because the man manifests no fear. He was probably merely repeating something he had heard from his jujitsu teacher.

"I see," said Okada with a laugh. "The policeman is the tiger and we three are drunks."

"*Silentium!*" commanded Ishihara as we turned the corner and approached the police box. From the corner we could see the policeman standing at the intersection.

Suddenly Ishihara, who was walking on the left, began addressing Okada. "Do you know the formula for finding the volume of a cone? You don't? Well, it's very easy. One-third of the area of the base times the height. So if the base is a circle, the volume will be one-third of the radius squared times pi times the height. If you know that pi is 3.1416, then it's simple. I learned pi as far as the eighth decimal place. Pi equals 3.14159265. If you remember that far, that's all you need for practical purposes."

We had passed the intersection. The policeman stood in front of the police box, which was on the left side of the street. He was looking at a rickshaw that was coming through Kayachō, headed in the direction of Nezu, and gave us no more than a meaningless glance.

"Why did you all of a sudden start talking about the volume of a cone?" I asked Ishihara, but at that instant I caught sight of the woman standing in the middle of the slope and looking this way. A feeling of strange agitation swept over me. All the time we had been making our way back from the north end of the pond I had been thinking more about the woman than about the police box. I don't know why, but I felt certain she would be waiting for Okada. And my hunch did not prove wrong. She had come several houses down from her own as though in greeting.

Taking care not to attract Ishihara's notice, I looked back and forth from the woman's face to Okada. Okada's customarily ruddy complexion had turned a deeper red and then, as though he were adjusting his cap, he touched his hand to the visor. The woman's face turned to stone and in her wide beautiful eyes was a look of infinite regret.

I could hear Ishihara making some reply to my question, but the meaning of his words did not penetrate my mind. Most likely he was explaining that the odd bulge in Okada's cloak had started him talking about the volume of a cone.

Ishihara too looked at the woman for a moment but apparently merely noted that she was attractive and then dismissed her completely from his mind. Presently he resumed his jabbering. "I explained to you the secret of maintaining stability of mind. But because you've had no proper training I was afraid that at the crucial moment you would be unable to put it into practice. So I employed a device to divert your minds in another direction. It wouldn't have mattered what I talked about, but as I just explained, I decided to talk about the formula for the volume of a cone. In any event, the device worked. Thanks to the formula for the volume of a cone, you were able to maintain the proper *unbefangen* attitude and get past the policeman without difficulty."

By this time the three of us had reached the Iwasaki mansion, where the road turns to the right. From there we entered an alley barely wide enough to allow two rickshaws to pass, so we were no longer in danger. Ishihara left Okada's side and walked ahead to guide us to his lodging. I looked back once, but the figure of the woman was no longer to be seen.

Okada and I stayed at Ishihara's place until late that night, mainly keeping Ishihara company while he ate wild goose and drank saké. Okada did not breathe a word about his forthcoming trip abroad, so I had no chance to ask him all the questions I had hoped to. Instead I sat listening while he and Ishihara exchanged stories about their experiences on the rowing team.

When I got back to the Kamijō I was too tired and drunk to sit up talking with Okada but went straight to bed. The next day when I returned from the university, I found that Okada had gone.

Thus, just as the one nail in the children's story precipitated a whole chain of events, so the fact that mackerel boiled in *miso* happened to be served at the Kamijō that evening kept Okada and Otama apart for all time. That was not the end of the affair, but the rest of the happenings lie outside the scope of my story of "The Wild Goose."

Now as I write the story I find that thirty-five years have passed since the events I relate. Half of the story derives from the period when I was on close terms with Okada. The other half comes from a time long after Okada's departure, when quite by chance I became acquainted with Otama and heard her description of what occurred. Just as two images combine in a stereoscope to form a single picture, so the events I observed earlier and those that were described to me later have been fitted together to make this story of mine.

Readers may perhaps ask how I came to know Otama and under what circumstances I heard her recital, but these matters too lie outside my story. I would only add that, needless to say, I am wholly lacking in the kind of qualifications that would fit me for the role of Otama's lover, so readers may spare themselves useless speculation on that point.

CPSIA information can be obtained at www.ICGtesting.com
264705BV00001B/2/P